A CRISIS OF LOVE AND JEALOUSY

BOOK ONE OF A JULIA LILLUS SERIES

JAMES ROBERTS

Edited by
JAMES ROBERTS
Illustrated by
JAMES ROBERTS

CONTENTS

DEDICATION

For those who have become victims of sexual assault.

For all who have suffered from a jealous partner.

And finally, to law enforcement and the court systems to bring justice where needed.

INTRODUCTION

"A Crisis Of Love And Jealousy" is a story about the deceit leading to physical assault, a romance involving erotic sex, physiological devastation, and murder. Each of these draws on the reader's emotions and challenges their judgments.

Throughout the book, the reader will explore the many facets of the personalities of the characters, and formulate opinions based on their beliefs and personal lives.

CHARACTERS

JOHN BAILEY

John, a resident of Cloverville, is a school music teacher and teaches music lessons for young children at his home. John Bailey is a pedophile, using his charm and cunningness to get closer and closer to the children, he is able to be alone with them during music lessons.

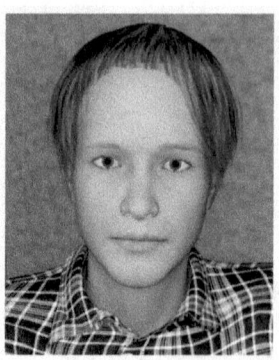

TIMOTHY LILLUS

Timothy, a resident of the town of Harford, is waking up from a restless night. He looks over at his wife, still sleeping, languishing in a silent and jealous rage. Timothy Lillus is a very suspicious man. He has nightmares that run through the entire night. They convince him that his wife is unfaithful to him. Timothy works hard on his jealous nature but can never seem to get past it every time he sees his wife out in public or when she is out with friends. He questions to whom she is seeing and why 'that guy' is looking at her. His wife is beautiful. Timothy knows any man would be more than happy to take her away from him. Timothy Lillus loves his wife but cannot get past the trust issue even though she will tell him she loves him very dearly and will never venture to another man.

Timothy, a slender man with reddish hair, is a laborer whose specialty is a pipe-fitter, especially steam piping. He is an expert, and he brings home a substantial paycheck which mimics his work. If one needs to repair a steam pipe, Timothy is the man for the job. At eighteen years of age, he was hired by Grapple Piping as a contractor to route the steam pipes in the Jackson City Prison.

JULIA LILLUS

Julia is waking from a restful sleep. As she opens her eyes, she notices her husband, Tim, through the open door in the bathroom. She gazes at his nude body, as he dresses for work, igniting a feeling in her the need for erotic intimacy.

Julia is a tall, beautiful, and a slender woman with a full head of long black hair. Her eyes are almond-shaped and her face heart-shaped, due to her Asian lineage, with a touch of a dimple in each of her cheeks. She has long slender, but toned legs.

Julia is a Deputy Officer for the Harford Police Department. She is a tough cop and loves her work. Tough cops need to endure what most humans do not or will not do, and Julia is no exception. She works out at the gym weekly with her ex-police friend Amanda.

Arriving at her home, after her workout, she greets Timothy with a passionate kiss even though it isn't always reciprocated by him.

Julia Lillus has occasional nightmares in her sleep with vivid thoughts, someday and somehow, she would have to make a snap decision that would haunt her the rest of her life.

THE BOYS

The boys awaken from sleep as soon as the sun rises. Both Tony and John anticipate another day filled with fun and adventures.

Tony and John are inseparable. They live in Cantor Square on the road with only one neighborhood house between theirs. In the summer, when school is out, one would see them together, sometimes at Tony's home and sometimes at John's home. At the ages of twelve, they have vivid imaginations. Tony always wants to be the secret agent while John, the villain. Sometimes they will switch roles. The boys hope their imaginative games will turn into reality someday.

Bicycles are their mode of transportation in the summer months while sledding down the hill around their homes is their winter mode of transportation. They spend hours together.

The road the boys live on is crossed by a railroad track further down where there is nothing but fields of tall grasses. Many times one can see them down at the railroad tracks picking up loose railway spikes or empty bottles of train lubricants. Innocence is always the atmosphere without a care in the world for those two.

RICHARD PELTZ

Richard is starting another day. Every morning, as he awakens, he looks forward to meeting Julia Lillus at the police station. Richard has a crush on her and fantasizes about being her lover, is mesmerized by her beauty, and is very protective of her. He knows she is out of reach for him due to her marriage to Timothy Lillus, but fantasizing about her is sufficient for the time being.

Richard Peltz is a Deputy Officer for the Harford Police Department and partners with deputy Bobbie Fritz. He is a good deputy and can be trusted to get the job done. His attention to detail is one of his greatest assets. Richard is the type of officer who will lay down his life for a fellow officer no matter the danger to him.

BOBBIE FRITZ

Bobbie is finishing up with her shower and finds her freshly cleaned uniform in her closet. As she is dressing, thoughts of Deputy Officer Richard Peltz crosses her mind.

Bobbie is infatuated with him and craves his attention. Knowing he has a crush on Julia Lillus, her chances are slim he will recognize her feelings.

Bobbie Fritz is a short redheaded, shapely, and beautiful Deputy for the Harford Police Department. At twenty-five years of age, Bobbie is the youngest officer in the police force.

Due to Richard's crush on Julia Lillus, it is difficult for Bobbie to work with him knowing she has little chance of him recognizing her feelings for him.

Bobbie is a caring deputy officer and usually sent to family disputes because of her caring personality.

RONNIE LACHOW

Ronnie is a nurse for the Jackson City Prison infirmary. Her looks and her age are very similar to Julia Lillus. Ronnie had been married at a young age, but it didn't last long. Since her divorce, she has been hesitant to start a relationship with a man, although she longs for the love and affection it brings. She can easily fall in love if she lets her guard down.

OFFICER ANGEL

Officer Angel, a thirty-two year old brunette, rises from her bed as the sunrise shines through her bedroom window. She is eager to start another day at the police station.

Angel is a Deputy Officer for the Harford Police Department. She is much like Julia Lillus almost to the point of being a clone. Although she is not a twin in the real sense to Julia, everything that she does is identical to Julia. Angel often partners up with officer Peltz in solving cases. At times, Richard Peltz is not sure if he is working with Julia or Angel.

FRANK ROLAND

Frank is sitting in his kitchen with his wife Edna, while reading the morning paper. He is finishing the last cup of coffee before he heads to the Harford Police Department.

Frank Roland is the Chief of Police for the Harford Police Department. He is an expert when it comes to law, and he does not cut corners. He knows his officers thoroughly. His deputies are family to him, and nothing will get in the way of their safety. Frank never sends a deputy on a case without a backup.

Retirement isn't far away, but that never diminishes his commitment to the community of Harford.

AMANDA SHORES

Amanda awakens upon sunrise and quickly puts on her Spandex®
pants, sweatshirt, and sneakers. After the protein shake, she leaves her
home to start her four-mile jog.

Amanda is a tall blond haired woman of thirty-two years of age.
She is beautiful, well toned and worked as a Police Officer in another
county. Her commitment to working out at the gym while being a cop
continues well into her departure from the police force.

She is a great friend to Julia Lillus and joins Julia in her weekly
workout routines at the gym every Wednesday night. After every
workout, she will drop Julia off at her home and waits until Julia is
safely inside. She often hesitates before driving off because Julia has
told her of Timothy's jealousy and usually an argument can be heard
as soon as Julia opens the door.

Amanda does not trust Timothy and is afraid that he, someday,
will hurt Julia.

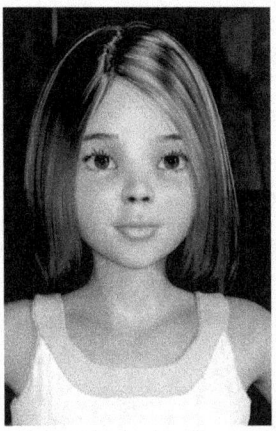

SARA DOWD

Sara, a ten year old girl, rises from her bed and begins to think about the clothes she will wear at school. Her closet is full of skirts, but she decides to pick out a pair of pants and a blouse. This has been her school attire since the 'incident'.

Sara Dowd is a typical child who attends the Elementary School in Cloverville. She is a happy-go-lucky kid, well-liked by her classmates, and volunteers at all school functions. Sara loves the piano and is taking lessons at the school.

JACKSON CITY PRISON

The light snow glistens on the tall pines surrounding the Jackson City Prison as the sun rises higher in the sky.

The prison is the largest in the state and located in a secluded area of the city. Canada is to the North for about 60 miles. Cantor Square and Harford are to the West and Cloverville to the East. The prison houses over 1000 inmates most of whom are murderers and rapists.

PREFACE

It is a cold winter day in the city of Harford. Timothy and Julia Lillus, are rising from a restful sleep. Julia, a Deputy Officer for the Harford Police Department is readying herself for another day at the office. Timothy gets dressed for his job at Carlson Plumbing and Pipe.

Amanda Shores has already begun her morning run. It is Wednesday and she is looking forward to her workout routine at the gym with Julia Lillus.

Richard Peltz, a Deputy Officer for the Harford Police Department rises thinking about Julia Lillus. They are partners in the Department, but Richard wishes they were partners outside of work.

Bobbie Fritz, a Deputy Officer, awakens to face another day at the Harford Police Department. Bobbie has a crush on Richard Peltz, but she can't find a way to show it to him. She is aware of his desire for Julia Lillus.

Frank Roland, the Chief of Police for the Harford Police Department sits at his kitchen table reading the morning newspaper. There is a court case being heard today, at the Cloverville Court House. Frank is relieved he won't be needed for this one.

John Bailey is due in court today at the Cloverville Court House. He is being put on trial for assault.

The city of Harford is quiet this morning. It appears the Police Department will have little to do today.

SAD TESTIMONY

I t was a cloudy day, Wednesday, in Cloverville and very cold. A winter storm is brewing from the West, and the forecast is lake effect snow off of Lake Ontario. The Cloverville Court House is bubbling over with voices of anger and contradictions.

"All rise! The court of Dowd versus Bailey is now in session, the Honorable Judge Newton presiding," the bailiff announces.

"Mr. Lewis, how does the defendant plead?" asks Judge Newton.

"The defendant pleads 'not guilty' your Honor."

"The prosecution calls Sara Dowd to the stand."

"Sara, you do know why you are here and you are to tell the truth?" asks Judge Newton.

"Yes, I do," Sara replies.

"Mr. Lowell, you may begin your line of questioning," says Judge Newton.

"Sara, if I may, please state your age."

"I am 10 years old."

"Sara, you are currently attending the Cloverville Elementary School?"

"Yes, I am."

"Sara can you describe what happened Friday the 12th of December at the time you were in class at the Cloverville Elementary School."

Sara responds, "I was asked by the music teacher to stop by his office after school so that he could tell me about a musical presentation. He wanted me to play the main character. After school, I went downstairs to his office with excitement. To be in the musical and be the lead character is what I had wished for such a long time. I knocked on the door; the music teacher told me to enter."

"Sara, what did you see?" asks attorney Lowell.

"The music teacher was sitting on the piano bench and asked me to sit down next to him...so...he...could explain...," as Sara starts to cry.

"That's OK, Sara, we can wait for you to compose yourself. I know this must be difficult for you. When you are ready, please continue," says the attorney.

"He asked me to sit next to him on the piano bench so that he could go over the script. I sat down next to him, and he started to tell me about the musical play. He said that he needed a very bright and pretty girl for the play and I was the perfect student to play the part. It was a Christmas Musical, and I would be playing the role of Santa Clause's head elf, and I would be wearing the elf suit which consisted of a pixie skirt, vest, hat and shoes with bells on the toes. I knew of that outfit because it had been used in other musicals...."

"Go on," says the attorney.

"He told me that I would need to come back in a few days for the fitting of the elf suit. As he was describing the role and going over the script, a page fell on the floor next to me. I bent down to pick it up, and suddenly I felt something touching my butt. He said he was sorry and his hand slipped while trying to keep me from falling off the piano bench. I continued to read the script with him, and then I felt his hand......go....up my skirt...oh, oh, oh....and he then slipped it between my legs......I...I..can't."

"That is fine, Sara, you do not need to go any further. Let me ask you one last question."

"Sara, is the music teacher that did these things to you in this courtroom at this time?"

"Yes," as she cries with tears running down her cheeks and pointing in the direction of the defendant's table. "Him! It was him, Mr. Bailey!"

The courtroom roars with voices of anger and disdain.

"Order! Order in this court!" exclaims Judge Newton. "Does the defense have questions for the plaintiff?"

"Yes, your Honor," answers defense attorney Lewis.

"You may begin," Judge Newton responds.

"Sara, I find it hard to believe that a school teacher who has been around many different aged children, such as you, could do such a thing. Young children at your age sometimes imagine things."

"Objection!" retorts attorney Lowell. "Your Honor, the defense is suggesting that the plaintiff is making this up."

"Objection sustained. The defense will stick to the facts and not enter leading suppositions," says Judge Newton.

"Sara, you stated that you were touched by Mr. Bailey. How and where did Mr. Bailey touch you?"

"Objection!" retorts attorney Lowell. "Your Honor, the plaintiff has already defined what happened in this case, and I see no need to have my client go into further detail. It is irrelevant."

"Objection sustained. Continue your line of questioning Mr. Lewis. Sara has already given enough detail of what happened to her," says Judge Newton.

"Sara, what did you do when Mr. Bailey placed his hand between your legs, as you say?" asks attorney Lewis.

"It all happened so fast, and I jumped up, and my underpants tore and partly came down my legs. I ran out of the room as fast as I could."

"So you say that your underpants were torn? Why?"

"All I can think he had a hold of them when I jumped up."

"Sara, did you tell your parents about Mr. Bailey touching you?"

"No, I...I... was too embarrassed, and thought that no one would believe me."

"Sara, did you continue as the main character of the Christmas Musical after this incident?"

"No, I did not and was not in the play at all."

"Thank you, Sara. I have no more questions."

"Mr. Lowell, are there any further questions?"

"Yes, your Honor, if I may."

"Please continue."

"Sara, is what you described here, the only time you had an encounter with Mr. Bailey?"

"No, I asked my mother if she would allow me to take private piano lessons. She said that she would enroll me in private lessons with Mr. Bailey because he was a school music teacher and offered private lessons at his home. I did not want to take music lessons with him, but I could not tell my mother why. I could not tell her what had happened that day in school. I told her I would go if she would go with me to the lessons."

"Why, Sara, didn't you tell your mother, then, about the encounter with Mr. Bailey?"

"I could not; I was scared. No one would believe me."

"Sara, you told me Mr. Bailey touched you again after he touched you in school. What happened? Was it during the private music lessons?"

"Yes."

"What happened, Sara?" questions attorney Lowell.

"Well, there was this one lesson."

"What day was this, Sara?"

"It was a Saturday, I think."

"OK, Sara, please continue."

"My mother had received a call on her cell phone. She did not want to interrupt my lesson, so she stepped outside to take the call. As soon as she went outside and while I was playing my Sonata, he...he..stood up next to me, unzipped his pants while grabbing at my hand to touch his private part."

"Sara, you are positive Mr. Bailey exposed his private part and tried to get you to touch him by grabbing your hand?"

"Yes, I am positive it is what happened."

The people in the courtroom roar in disbelief.

"Order! Order in this court! If there are more outbursts in this court, you will be dismissed," states Judge Newton.

"Are there more questions from the prosecution?"

"No, your Honor, no more questions from the prosecution."

"Does the defense have any questions for the plaintiff?" asks Judge Newton.

"Yes, I do, your Honor."

"Sara, you have told us quite a story. I find it hard to believe that Mr. Bailey exposed himself to you. Sara, after listening to your story, I can't help to wonder if you are a little girl who wanted him to do the things to you that you describe."

"Objection!"

"Objection sustained. The jury will disregard."

"Continue, Mr. Lewis, and let me warn you that your line of questioning is suggestive. You must stick to the facts of this case."

"Yes, your Honor," states attorney Lewis.

"Sara, you say that Mr. Bailey unzipped his pants and wanted you to touch him?"

"Yes, he did."

"Tell me, did this happen before your mother returned into the house?"

"No, this happened just as my mother returned into the house."

"Sara, if Mr. Bailey had exposed himself to you before your mother returned into the house, would have you pulled away from him?"

"He did that just as my mother was returning. I did not ask for it," Sara cries with tears running down her cheeks.

"Objection! Your Honor, the defense is trying to insinuate that the plaintiff wanted the advances of Mr. Bailey," states attorney Lowell.

"Objection sustained."

"Your Honor, the defense is just trying to define the plaintiff's feelings for my client, Mr. Bailey," states attorney Lewis.

"I believe that the plaintiff's feelings were discovered," says Judge Newton.

"The defense rests. No more questions."

"Thank you, Sara, you may step down," Judge Newton states.

"I call the witness Mrs. Dowd to the stand," states attorney Lowell.

"Mrs. Dowd, please take the stand."

"Mrs. Dowd, do you solemnly swear to tell the truth and nothing but the truth so help you God?" asks the bailiff.

"Yes, I do," Vivian Dowd replies.

"Please be seated."

"Mrs. Dowd, what is your relationship to the plaintiff?" asks attorney Lowell.

"I am Sara's mother."

"Mrs. Dowd, did you accompany your daughter, on a Saturday, to her music lesson?"

"Yes, I did."

"Where was this music lesson?"

"It was a private music lesson and in the home of Mr. Bailey."

"Did you always accompany your daughter, Sara, at these music lessons?"

"Yes."

"Why, Mrs. Dowd?"

"I accompanied my daughter because she asked me to."

"Did Sara tell you why she wanted you to go to the music lessons with her?"

"No, but it is understandable that a girl of ten years of age would want someone to be with her when she was alone in a home with a male stranger."

"Mrs. Dowd, did you trust Mr. Bailey?"

"Yes, at the time I did."

"Mrs. Dowd, on that day of the music lesson, please tell me what happened."

"Sara was playing her Sonata at the piano."

"Where was Mr. Bailey at that time?"

6

"He was sitting next to Sara on the piano bench like always, directing her."

"Describe to me, Mrs. Dowd, what followed."

"I received a phone call on my cell phone that I had to answer. You see, I am a nurse, and I have to be on call certain days. I went outside to answer the call so that I would not interfere with Sara's lesson."

"How long were you outside?"

"I was outside for maybe two to three minutes."

"What happened when you returned into Mr. Bailey's house?"

"I opened the door, and Mr. Bailey was standing next to Sara with his pants unzipped and pulling Sara's hand towards his exposed area."

"What happened next?"

"Sara was in tears and pulled herself away from Mr. Bailey, and we rushed to the car and immediately called 911."

"Mrs. Dowd, did Sara ever tell you what had happened to her when she was in school?"

"Yes, as soon as we got in the car and on the way to our home, she told me all of the details and…and…I felt so sorry for her….I am so..so…sorry. I should have known. I blame myself."

"Your Honor, I don't have anymore questions," states attorney Lowell.

"Does the defense wish to question the witness?" asks Judge Newton.

"Yes," states attorney Lewis.

"Mrs. Dowd, you say that you trusted my client, Mr. Bailey and why is that?"

"Mr.Bailey is a music teacher in the Cloverville Elementary School, and I had heard nothing about Mr. Bailey that would lead me to mistrust him. It is why I enrolled Sara into private lessons with him."

"Mrs. Dowd were there any times during Sara's music lessons where you had seen inappropriate advances or gestures to Sara from Mr. Bailey?"

"No."

"Had Sara ever given signs that she had problems with Mr.

Bailey?"

"No."

"I find it hard to believe that my client, Mr. John Bailey, would risk exposing himself to Sara when you were right outside the door and could re-enter at any time."

"Mrs. Dowd, please tell the court what you saw as you entered the music room after your phone call."

"I opened the door, and Mr. Bailey was standing up."

"Was my client-facing Sara or facing you?"

"Mr. Bailey was on the right of Sara next to the piano bench and facing her. Sara was facing the piano. In an instant, while he had his pants unzipped, his penis popped out, and he grabbed Sara's hand and pulled it to that area."

"Mrs. Dowd, are you sure that you saw my clients pants unzipped?"

"Yes, they were unzipped, and he was exposing himself." "What did Mr. Bailey do when he saw you come into the room from outside?"

"He stepped away from Sara facing me from the piano." "Were my client's pants unzipped then?"

"No, it looked like he had zipped them back up."

"So, Mrs. Dowd, you could have been mistaken that my clients pants were unzipped?"

"No! I know what I saw, and they were unzipped in front of Sara!"

"No more questions, the defense rests," states attorney Lewis.

"I call the defendant to the stand," requests attorney Lowell.

"Mr. Bailey, do you solemnly swear to tell the truth and nothing but the truth so help you God?" asks the bailiff.

"Yes, I do," John Bailey replies.

"Please be seated."

"Mr. Bailey, did the Cloverville Elementary School Board ever approach you about any incidents that involved the students and you."

"No, there never were any incidents, and they did not mention anything to me."

"Mr. Bailey, am I correct in saying you know Sara as a student in the Cloverville Elementary School?"

"Yes."

"Mr. Bailey, did you select Sara for the Christmas Musical to play the part of the head elf because she was pretty and attractive?"

"Objection! Your Honor, the prosecution is insinuating that my client picked the plaintiff for the musical because of her looks."

"Objection sustained."

"Your Honor the prosecution is trying to decipher why Mr. Bailey picked Sara for the musical," says attorney Lowell.

"Mr. Lowell, keep in line with the facts and do not imply anything to the contrary," states Judge Newton.

"Mr. Bailey, did you select Sara for the lead part in the Christmas Musical?"

"Yes, Sara was very eager to be in the play."

"Mr. Bailey, how did she perform her part in the musical?"

"She didn't. At the last minute, she decided to not be in the play."

"So, why is that, Mr. Bailey?"

"I don't know. I couldn't figure it out."

"Mr. Bailey, Sara has stated that during one of her music lessons, and I believe it was the same time that you were discussing the musical with her, you had reached under her dress. Can you explain this, Mr. Bailey?"

"I do not remember it as Sara describes. Many times during a music lesson a student may feel that I possibly touched them where they didn't want. Both the student and I sit on the piano bench and students, being young and nervous while performing their lessons correctly, squirm around quite a bit. She may have hit or touched a part of me and maybe, in this case, my hand, with her body and believed that it was I who touched her."

"So, Mr. Bailey, I hear you telling me that Sara probably moved and your hand happened to be in the way as her dress covered your hand?"

"Yes, that is correct, but my hand was never under her dress."

"Mr. Bailey, could a student squirm, as you say, around enough to say they were touched in an inappropriate manner under a dress?"

"No, I can't see how that could be possible."

"Mr. Bailey, Sara stated that you placed your hand between her legs during the same time that maybe your hand ended up under her dress due to her possibly squirming, but you say that it couldn't be possible. Is that correct Mr. Bailey?"

"Yes, I never touched Sara anywhere intentionally."

"Mr. Bailey, could a student rip their underwear by squirming during a music lesson?"

"It doesn't seem possible."

"Sara had said that her underpants were coming down her legs when she left the music lesson and discovered they were ripped."

"I do not recall seeing Sara's underwear coming down her legs when she left the lesson."

"Mr. Bailey, it appears that Sara had made an impression on you."

"Sara was a special student, wasn't she? She was the best student for the lead part. Sara was so excited to be the lead and eager to learn the script. She was just who you wanted for the musical out of all of the other students. Am I correct, Mr. Bailey? She was so special..."

"Objection!"

"Mr. Bailey, you reached under her dress while she was reading the script and then fondled her with your hand between her legs as she sat there; grabbed her underwear and ripped them as she jumped up pulling them down her legs...."

"Objection!"

"Is this true, Mr. Bailey?"

"No, you got it all wrong! She was a beautiful girl for her age, but I......"

"Mr. Bailey, I would like to now switch to when Sara was taking private lessons with you; specifically a Saturday lesson in January?"

"I can't remember any Saturday lessons with Sara."

"Mr. Bailey, you say that you do not remember, but Sara and her mother remember that day. How many questions do I need to ask you before you miraculously remember the lesson in question?"

"I have many student lessons, and I cannot remember the dates or what students I have had lessons on particular dates."

"Mr. Bailey, during your detainment, you willfully gave the court your student lesson journal and did you know who we found in your journal? We found Sara Dowd in your journal, and we even read that you had a lesson with Sara on Saturday the 20th of January."

"OK, it must be so, but I do not remember that specific lesson with Sara."

"Mr. Bailey, I am not going to waste the courts time or your time, so I am going to get to the facts. You had said that Sara was beautiful for her age."

"Therefore, it stands to reason that she continued to make an impression on you. Mr. Bailey, can you recall what Sara was wearing at the time of the music lesson?"

"No, not exactly."

"Sara was wearing slacks and a long sleeve shirt according to her mother's statement."

"Objection! I see no reason to discuss what the plaintiff wore during the music lesson," states attorney Lewis.

"Mr. Lowell?"

"Your Honor, I am trying to make a point, here."

"Please get on with it, then, Mr. Lowell. Objection overruled," says Judge Newton.

"Mr. Bailey taking into account your statements during the prior questioning and those of Mrs. Dowd and Sara, it appears your obsession with Sara had grown so much…."

"Objection!"

"….because she didn't have a skirt on…."

"Objection!"

"…and you were unable to grab her panties, you decided to…."

"Objection!"

"…to unzip your pants, expose yourself, and to force her to touch you…"

"Objection!"

"Mr. Lowell!" exclaims Judge Newton.

"No further questions your Honor. The prosecution rests."

"Does the defense have questions for Mr. Bailey?"

"The defense rests, your Honor."

THE SENTENCING

In the Judge's chambers, the jury has assembled. They deliberate in conversation.

—"You know he was after that little girl in the elementary school. Kids don't rip their underwear."

"Yeah, he even said that she was beautiful for her age."

"It appears that if she hadn't run out of the office, he would have advanced on her further."

"But, think about the time when she was at that music lesson and what she claimed he did. Exposed himself!"

"If she was infatuated with the music teacher as the defense wants us to believe, why would she complain about his advances?"

"No, I believe that he did expose himself to her and her mother even witnessed it. He fits the description and characterization of a pedophile."—

"All rise! The court of Dowd versus Bailey is now in session, the Honorable Judge Newton presiding," the bailiff announces.

"Mr. John Bailey, please rise."

"Has the jury made a decision?" asks Judge Newton.

"Yes, your Honor, we have. The jury has given a verdict of guilty."

"Mr. Bailey, we have heard your testimony and the testimonies of your accuser and the witness. In all of the times that I have served this court, I cannot think of a time when I have had to hear the most inexcusable actions you have forced on this young lady. She is supposed to be protected by you, the teacher, and the faculty of the school system. Shame on the school system for not acting, and shame on you, Mr. Bailey. May God have mercy for your soul! The court finds you guilty of assaulting a minor and student with the intent of touching her genitals, exposing yourself to a minor, and inappropriately touching a child while acting as a school teacher. Your name will be recorded in the national database as a pedophile, and I sentence you to 15 years in the Jackson City Prison. The court is dismissed!"

TIMOTHY AND JULIA

There is a ceremony Julia and Timothy are attending at the Church of Christ.

"Timothy Lillus, do you take Julia Barnes to be your lawfully wedded wife in sickness and health, for richer or poorer, till death do you part?"

"I do."

"Julia Barnes, do you take Timothy Lillus to be your lawfully wedded husband in sickness and health, for richer or poorer, till death do you part?"

"I do."

"By the power of God, I pronounce you man and wife."

"You may kiss the bride."

"How does it feel to be Mrs. Julia Lillus?" asks Timothy.

"It is just beautiful! Tim, I have waited for this day to come and now it is finally here," answers Julia.

"I love you so much, Julia."

"Tim, I am hoping that you believe me when I tell you how much I love you and not be jealous of other men who might strike a conversation with me during the reception."

"I am OK, sweetheart. I believe that my jealous streak is well needed at times. I never want to share you with another man."

"Just remember, Tim, just because a man may be conversing with me, it does not mean that I am falling out of love with you. You should have enough trust in me to never have to worry about it."

"Yeah, I know, Julia, but don't you think that a little bit of jealousy is healthy?"

"I have to admit that knowing you are a little jealous, at times, makes me feel you want to be with me and definitely don't want to share me with another man. It does make me feel I am protected by you."

"See, Julia, that is what I mean."

"Yes, Tim, but letting it get out of hand will smother me from society."

"No, Julia, I will never do that to you."

"Come here, Tim! Hold me, please."

"I will do better than that. Do we have any time before we need to show up at the reception?"

"Timothy Lillus what do you have in mind? Why do you ask?"

"I can see that you mean business...unzipping the back of my dress...and what? Unhooking my bra! Tim, I do not think we have any time for this. Besides, what I have in store for you will take quite a bit of time and I do not want to be distracted by lack of time."

"C'mon, Tim, you need to leave my garter on for the activities at the reception."

"Julia, I am readjusting it. I believe that it is not in the correct position."

"It is you devil....oh...oh..Tim, stop it! All I need is to be going to that reception sweating and disheveled…mmmm.mmm..oh..oh. Now you did it, Tim! Ah…ah…"

"Are you happy now? My pussy is throbbing!" exclaims Julia.

"Well, Julia, how does it feel to get your first orgasm?"

"All right, just get your fingers out of there and let my dress down. I told you we will wait until later. I do love you so much, Tim."

"I would like to announce the arrival of Mr. and Mrs. Timothy Lillus!" announces the DJ at the reception.

"We will start off, first, with the bride and groom's dance."

"Tim, you had to go and get me to 'cum'," Julia whispers in Tim's ear during their dance.

"I can't stop thinking about it and my pussy is still throbbing."

"Good, Julia, I guess you will be ready for me, later, tonight."

"Tim, I have been ready for you…your..you know, long before this day."

"Julia, I have enough trouble keeping myself…well, ya know… behaving, while gazing at you, I don't need to have you stir me up even more with your sexual jargon. You can feel aroused and pretty much no one, here, will realize it, but as far as me being aroused, they all will be able to see that. Let's talk about the home we find and what city our home will be in," says Timothy.

"OK, Tim, can we have a mirror installed on the ceiling above our bed?"

"Julia Marie! What am I to do with you?" asks Timothy.

"Well, Tim, I cannot believe you are saying you don't know what you are going to do with me!" exclaims Julia.

"Mrs. Julia Lillus, I will show you tonight!"

AFTER THE WEDDING AND AT TIM AND JULIA'S HOME

"Tim, I am going to the gym to workout. I need to tone up for the new job at the Police Department."

"OK, be careful, there are some brutes there, just looking for women."

"Yeah, I know, Tim. Please do not worry. I will be all right. Watch that jealous streak of yours, Tim."

AFTER A YEAR OR SO, JULIA QUESTIONS TIM

"Tim, what are your thoughts about having a family? I think I would like to have a baby."

"Have a baby?"

"Yeah, we have been married for over a year, and I think it is time."

"Well, Julia, I don't think I am ready for that."

"Come on, Tim, why not?"

"I don't think I know how, Julia."

"What? You don't know what to do to give me a baby? It is easy, just keep penetrating me, and I will take care of the rest."

"No, Julia, that is not what I meant. I mean I am not sure whether I can share you at this time."

"Tim, I am worried about you."

"Why is that, Julia?"

"I have noticed that you are becoming more and more jealous of me. It is not normal, Tim. You are starting to smother me. You have to believe I will still love you even if we have children. You need to trust in me to know I am not looking for other men. Would you be willing to go to the doctor for a checkup?"

"Julia, I really don't think there is anything wrong with me. It's just

17

that the more I am around you, the more I see your beauty, and I am sure that others see it too."

"Timothy Lillus! I love you and only you! Now take my hand and follow me to our bedroom. Please call the doctor tomorrow and make an appointment. I want to be sure that you are OK. I can't stand the thought of you not being here with me."

"Sweetheart, I am not going to die, and I will call to make the appointment."

Timothy quickly changes the subject of the conversation and says, "Now come over here!" He gently pushes Julia down on the bed. "Off go the panties!"

"What do you think, Tim?" asks Julia as she grabs each of her ankles with her hands while spreading her legs.

"Oh, such a sweet sight staring at me," says Tim as he bends down to kiss her.

TIM AND JULIA ARRIVE AT THE DOCTOR'S OFFICE

"Doctor Brandt, this is my lovely wife, Julia Lillus."

"Nice to meet you Mrs. Lillus. What can I do for you Mr. Lillus?"

"Excuse me Tim, but doctor, may I tell you what seems to be happening with Tim according to the way I am experiencing it?"

"Yes, Mrs. Lillus"

"Doctor, you can call me by my name."

"OK, Julia, what seems to be the problem?"

"Tim and I have been married for a little over a year. In the very beginning, Tim was known to have a bit of a jealous streak in him. I did not think much about it in the beginning because I know it is a typical human emotion, not the best I may add. Tim's jealousy has progressively gotten worse up to now where his trust for me is not there."

"What do you mean, Julia?"

"Doctor, I expressed my interest to Tim that I would like to have children. His response to that was he did not want to share me. I can't go to the gym without Tim thinking that men, there, are hitting on me. I cannot go anywhere in public without Tim thinking that I have enticed a man in some fashion. I fear that it will be not long before he swears that I am having affairs."

"Mr. Lillus, I mean Tim, what is your response to Julia's experiences?"

"Doctor, she is correct in noticing my jealousy, but I feel that it is a natural thing."

"How, Tim?"

"Julia is beautiful...more so than most women, and I have to protect her from men who recognize her beauty. They could take advantage of her."

"I see. Why don't you want to give Julia children?"

"I know children need a lot of attention from the mother and I can't be without her for that long."

"Be without her, Tim? What do you mean?"

"Doc, I can't abstain that long from...you know, Doc."

"Tim, you are afraid that your chances to have sex with Julia will stop when she has children? Do you think that Julia would want to stop having sex with you?"

"I would have to share her. It would be hard for me to have to share her."

"Tim, without going further into this, because it is the job for a counselor, most all females with children don't stop having intimate relations with their husbands because of the children interfering, as you say. Females want sex as much as you and many may want it more than their husbands."

"Doctor, do you think that Tim's issue is self-centeredness and selfishness?" asks Julia.

"Julia, I really do not believe so. I feel that it is deeper than that. I believe that he has symptoms of an Affliction called Othello's Syndrome."

"What is that Doctor Brandt?" asks Tim.

"The syndrome's basis is jealousy; deep jealousy to the point of mistrusting, particularly in your case, you Julia. A person with this affliction believes that they need someone so much that they want them all to themselves and believe that the partner, you, in this case, is purposely escalating the jealousy by triggers such as affairs, flirting, hitting on, etc."

"Doctor, I am not having an affair and certainly not alluring men!"

"Of course not, Julia, but Tim may feel this way due to the syndrome affecting his reasoning. The unfortunate thing is, Julia, this syndrome cannot be cured. It can be treated, but not cured. In many cases, it can escalate, without treatment, to a point where he could cause you physical harm."

"What treatment choices does Tim have, doctor?"

"There is medication, but I do not believe in that treatment because the side effects can make the issue worse. I do believe in counseling, and it does work. Counseling of six months to a year usually is enough for the inflicted to learn to control their jealousy to normalcy."

"What is normalcy, doctor?"

"Julia, normalcy is the amount of jealousy that normal humans carry around with them. We all, you and I, have a certain amount of jealousy."

"Doctor, I would like to interject that I believe I do not have this syndrome that you describe," says Tim.

"Tim, I am sorry, I do not agree with you. If you love Julia as much as you profess, you will not put her through this. I believe she has had enough and you need treatment."

"Tim, will you go to counseling for me? For us?" asks Julia.

"Yes, sweetheart, I will."

TIMOTHY MAKES AN APPOINTMENT FOR COUNSELING

"Hello, Timothy Lillus. You are here, today, to start the journey in learning how to control your jealousy and prevent jealous rages. I need to ask you, are you willing to do what it takes to obtain control? It is going to take a lot of work, and it will be uncomfortable at times."

"Yes, Mr. Haas, I am willing."

"Good, now let's start. Why, Timothy, do you mistrust your wife?"

"Do you see how beautiful she is? I should be jealous!"

"Timothy, you must think beyond yourself. You must start believing that your relationship with your wife is a mutual relationship. Don't you think that she has a part in your relationship, your marriage, to be true to you? This is where trust starts. Timothy, I am sure that your wife proves her love to you, doesn't she?"

"Yes, she does."

"How does she, Timothy?"

"Well, she tells it to me all of the time. She shows it to me, too."

"How does she show it, Timothy?"

"Well, she is more than willing to have sex; she lives for it and initiates it a lot."

"OK, that certainly is one way, but have you ever seen her with other men? Have you ever seen anything about her actions which would make you think that she is 'going out' on you?"

"Well, no, Mr. Haas."

"Good, this is where we are going to start."

AFTER A FEW WEEKS OF COUNSELING

"Tim will you be going to counseling today?"

"No, Julia, I am all done with the sessions. I am cured!"

"Tim, it has only been a month. Remember what Doctor Brandt told us. The counseling takes six months to a year or maybe even more."

"Mr. Haas tells me he is certain that I can handle my jealousy now."

"Well, OK, Tim, but if you feel yourself slipping, please go back to counseling."

"Yes, Julia; yes, I will."

"Good morning sweetheart, I feel so good, and I don't have to go to work. Do you have to go to work today?" asks Timothy.

"Nope, I have today off. What do you want to do today, Tim?" asks Julia.

"Oh, Tim, I think I know what that stare means."

"What stare?" asks Timothy.

"Well, it appears that your eyes are affixed on the crotch of my teddy I am wearing, and it looks as if something else has awakened on you," says Julia.

THE AFFAIR

At the gym, Julia and Amanda are finishing their workout routines.

"Amanda, that was such a great workout! I burned up the carbs tonight," says Julia.

"You sure did," replies Amanda.

"I am going to take a shower. I don't know, but this burn I am feeling from such a great workout will probably last all the way home. I do not think that a shower will stop my sweating," Julia said as she ventures into the ladies bathroom.

As Julia removes her clothes and steps into the shower, water running over her body, her nipples become erect and she reaches down with her finger to tease her clit saying to herself, "Oh, I can't wait to see Tim. We are going to have hot sex tonight!"

AFTER HER WORKOUT, JULIA SHOWERS AND CHANGES INTO A CLEAN PAIR

OF SPANDEX® PANTS AND A DRY SPORTS BRA , BECAUSE IT TURNS TIM ON
TO SEE HER COME HOME WEARING THEM. ON HER WAY HOME, SHE ENTERS
INTO CONVERSATION WITH AMANDA

"Amanda, I do not know what I am going to do about Tim." "Why, Julia, what is the problem with Tim?"

"You know, I have spoken about his problem with you in the past."

"Oh, no, is he getting worse with his jealousy?" asks Amanda.

"Yes, he is. He does not trust me to go anywhere alone and even when he goes places with me; he is determined to think that I am trying to draw men to me like a magnet. I love Tim with all of my heart and do not want to be with anyone else but him. He is now thinking that I am having an affair with someone."

"It is too bad he doesn't realize what he has and believes how you feel about him. You are so beautiful, Julia. For you to only want to be with him, is special. He doesn't know what he has in your relationship," states Amanda.

"Amanda, I am beginning to become afraid of him. I feel that if he gets much worse, he will harm me in some fashion."

"Can you get some help for him. Maybe a counselor?"

"He has been to a counselor. I have tried to get him to go back, but he swears that he doesn't have a problem. He says the problem is me drawing men to myself, and then, having an affair with them."

"Julia, I am here for you and anything that I can do for you, you know I would."

"Amanda, from now on when you drop me off at my home, please wait a few minutes to make sure that Tim doesn't try to harm me. I may be a cop and tough, but I still fear Tim."

"Thanks for the ride home, Amanda," says Julia.

"No problem, I will just wait a few minutes to be sure that you get in without any altercations."

"Hello, Tim, I am home!" Julia shouts as she opens the door to her home. Tim is sitting in a chair watching the television and looks up as Julia approaches.

"I have been waiting for you to come home," Timothy retorts in anger. "I have just about had it with you coming home from a supposed workout class. I know what you have been doing. Just look at you with that sports bra, and you look very provocative in those Spandex® pants. I can see your entire body shape as if you were wearing no clothes at all. Your hair is all wet, and you are sweating. I'll bet he did you good!"

"Timothy, what on earth are you talking about? I have been over this with you. Amanda and I go out Wednesday evenings to the gym to workout. After my workout, I take a shower and because I have a full head of hair and it is long, it does not dry any too fast. I am sweating because I had a great workout and the burn is still with me. You need to get a hold of your jealousy, Tim! You should know that I love you and would never leave you for another man. And as far as provocative, you told me that I look sexy to you when I wear these clothes. So, I wear these so that it is the first thing you see when I come in the door. Tim, please come here and hold me. I want to show you how much I love and adore you."

"So, you think that I want to come over to you when you have just been with another man?" asks Timothy.

———

TIMOTHY HAS RAISED HIS VOICE SO MUCH THAT AMANDA CAN HEAR THE ARGUMENT FROM HER CAR. SHE DECIDES TO GO TO THE DOOR

———

"Hey Julia, it is Amanda. Is everything all right?" "Amanda, please come in. The door is not locked. Amanda, will you please explain to Tim where I, we, have been tonight?"

"Timothy Lillus why don't you listen to your wife? Julia has told you over and over that she and I go to the gym every Wednesday night to do our workout routines. You know Julia has to keep up her endurance to perform her job as a Police Officer, and a damn good one too! Timothy, look at our gym membership cards. You will notice that both Julia's card and my card have been punched tonight. You saw me pick Julia up tonight to go to the gym and now you see that I brought her back. She has been with me the entire night. Timothy, do you think I would bother trekking your wife around town if she is having an affair? Do you think I would wait around for Julia to finish with her 'man', who you keep saying she is having an affair, to take her home afterward? Come on Timothy Lillus think about it."

"Amanda, I am OK, now. Thanks for dropping me off and I will see you next Wednesday for another great workout!"

Amanda leaves the Lillus's home to return to her home.

HOT SEX

As soon as Amanda leaves, Julia quickly grabs the moment to entice Timothy into having sex with her.

"Tim, we are alone, and I am in the mood for some intimacy. How about you? Are you convinced that I haven't been with a man tonight?"

"I guess so, yes," Timothy answers sheepishly.

"The only man that I will be with tonight is you, Tim. I love you so much."

Tim draws Julia to his chest and begins to kiss her as she reaches toward his groin. Immediately there is a response, and she feels his hardness in her hand. Tim, then, starts to gently lift Julia's sports bra up over her breasts. "I love how hard you become just with my touch," as Julia pushes her hand down into his undershorts and wraps her hand around his penis.

"I love how firm your breasts are," as Tim takes a firm but gentle grasp of one and then the other. He places his lips around her nipples and starts to suck on them gently, caressing them as his tongue dances around them. "Mmm," moans Julia.

Julia slips out of her Spandex® pants as Tim removes his pants and shorts. Julia lies down on the bed as Tim lowers himself onto her. Tim reaches and begins to place his fingers into her pussy while caressing her clitoris.

"Julia, you are so wet."

"Hmm. I know. Please lick me!"

Tim slides down between her legs as he gently spreads them and places his head between them. He starts pressing his tongue into her pussy's slit and into her love tunnel. He tastes her wetness, which is now freely flowing from her arousal.

"Oh…oh..hmmm.hmmm..oh.ooh," moans Julia.

Tim continues very slowly, tongue into the slit, in an upward motion towards Julia's clit. Once there, his tongue dances ever so lightly on the tip of it.

"Ah…ah….ah..Tim, Tim, I can't stand it! I…I…I…oh..oh…," Julia climaxes and her pussy throbs as her heart beats rapidly.

Tim continues with his tongue with one last lick of her slit and continues up, licking her pubic hairs straight to her navel; gently up over her abdomen, sucking on and licking her skin. Julia feels Tim's hardness pass into the slit of her pussy as he progresses upward on her body to reach her breasts.

"Honey, your nipples are so large and erect," he quietly states as he positions his lips once more on each one and allows his tongue to dance on them.

"Ahhhhhhhhhhhhh…," screams Julia in ecstasy as she once again climaxes.

Tim slowly moves to a position that allows him access to Julia's pussy, and she, his penis. He sticks his tongue in as he tastes her wetness. Julia places his hardness into her mouth and begins to suck.

"You taste so sweet, as he licks her slit of her pussy while his tongue reaches in, and he starts to suck on her clit."

"You are so thick and long," Julia says as she continues to suck, and then moves her mouth to engulf his testicles.

Tim rises and re-positions himself so that he can thrust his hardness into Julia as he starts to suckle her breasts, this time in a rhythmic fashion, first one and then the other.

"Thrust slower, Tim, and ride up onto my clit. Yes, that's it..oh..oh…mmmm," Julia moans.

Tim thrusts with a certain rhythm which begs Julia to move her body in concert. Julia cannot believe how wet she is. She can feel her wetness running out and down past her ass and onto her cheeks.

Tim begins to feel pressure building deep inside his groin which pleasures him to thrust a little faster. At the same time, Julia's clit is aroused to the point of climax.

"Tim, I think I am going to 'cunm'. Oh…oh.mmm.mmm, my clit throbs each time you thrust your cock into me!"

"I…I'm almost there, Julia. Let me know when you reach climax, and I will release into you."

"Oh….oh…oh, yes…yes…yes," Julia moans. "Ohooooooo…"

Julia climaxes as she feels a release of her wetness spraying out of her vagina. Tim had hit her "G" spot while thrusting causing the eruption.

"Ah…ah…ah…oh…oh," pants Tim with an increased heart rate as he anticipates his release.

Tim reels as he feels his load travel and blasts out and into its target. Julia feels the sudden warmth of his release into her love tunnel. She 'cums' one after another.

Tim rolls off of Julia, and for a moment they both lie breathing hard, sweating and resting with exhaustion. Both of them feel satisfied as Tim's penis continues to throb from his release and Julia, with her pelvis throbbing, senses his release leaking out between her legs down to her ass.

After a short time, Tim rolls back towards Julia and gestures with his caresses for her to roll onto her stomach. Julia turns over, and Tim grasps her hips and draws them up to him as he kneels on the bed and looks at Julia's pussy, still throbbing and dilated from penetration. His penis begins to get hard, and inserts his tongue into her slit, while kissing it. He, then, runs his finger up to her clit as he slowly, but rhythmically massages it, and pushes his other fingers in an out of her love tunnel.

"Oh, oh, mm.mm., fuck me, Tim," Julia moans. As his finger dances on her clit, she senses her inevitable climax.

Julia, still aroused from the previous penetration, and Tim's rhythmic touch to her clit, immediately starts to climax, but this time the climax continues. One orgasm after another and another.

"Oh, oh, Tim, ah, ah, mm, mm, I am going to 'cum'! Fuck me, fuck me hard!"

Tim senses her satisfaction and thrusts his penis into her, penetrating deeply, as her wetness reciprocates. Julia does not care how fast Tim is pushing because of her consistent climaxes. She feels a sort of numbness, but can still feel Tim's hardness swelling with each thrust of his rhythm.

"Ah, mm," moans Julia. Tim continues to thrust deeply. "Ah, ah, oh, it's coming…ah..ah, Julia! I can't stop it…it's coming. I can feel it traveling…ah……." With one last thrust, Tim's penis blasts its release into Julia.

"Oh……Oh…," moans Tim as he gently lowers his himself onto Julia's throbbing body and they share a passionate kiss intertwining their tongues. Tim slowly rolls to her side as his swollen penis slides out of her vagina.

"Tim, that was out of this world," says Julia, panting and soaking wet from sweat, as her entire pelvis is writhing with a rhythmic and pleasurable numbness.

JULIA AND TIM, ONCE AGAIN, LIE ON THE BED EXHAUSTED SATISFACTORILY. THEY CUDDLE EACH OTHER WITH TIM SNUGGLING BETWEEN JULIA'S BREASTS AND HER GENITALS INVITING ANOTHER ENTRANCE WITH HER LEG SLUMPED OVER TIM'S THIGH. THEY SLEEP WITHOUT WAKING UNTIL MORNING

AS JULIA AWAKENS IN THE MORNING, SHE HOPES IT IS A NEW BEGINNING FOR TIM AND HER.
TIM DREAMT ALL NIGHT THAT MAYBE JULIA WOULD END HER PROVOCATIVENESS WITH OTHER MEN

———

THE CRIME

A couple of weeks has passed since Tim and Julia had hot sex. Tonight, Julia and Tim decide they will go out to dinner. They haven't been out together for a long time because of Timothy's jealousy.

"Julia, I am starting to believe you will never find another man to replace me."

"Oh, come on Tim, I keep telling you that over and over. Why do you finally think that way?"

"The sex we had the other night is encouraging to me. I am beginning to feel that I am the only man in your life. I don't think that you would perform like that with another man like you did with me."

"Come on, Tim! You should know you are my man. You are my husband. I married you because I love you. I hope you will remember this when you start feeling your jealous rage."

"We can make love as often as you like if it helps you to trust me. I truly love you, and only you! I will never get tired of you and I making love to each other, Tim."

TIM AND JULIA ARRIVE AT THE RESTAURANT FOR DINNER

As Julia and Tim are having their dinner, a couple of men enter the restaurant. Julia immediately recognizes them. They come to the gym regularly when she and Amanda are there for their workout routines. They haven't approached Julia or Amanda while at the gym, but Julia has noticed these two guys always trying to hit upon the teenagers.

"Good thing that I am older," Julia says quietly under her breath. "Tim would revert right back to his problem with jealousy if they approached me at the gym as they do the young teenage girls. Those guys want the young, naive ones; easier to get into their panties. Oh, crap, why should I be thinking that way? It must be a remnant from the hot sex Tim and I had a few weeks ago."

"Hey, look here," the two guys remark as they approach Julia and Tim's table.

"Do I know you?" Tim asks.

"Hell, no, but we know this babe! Do you know she comes to the gym regularly and does her workout routines precisely every Wednesday night at 8:00 pm? We like those moves you do, honey! The gyration of your ass puts your cunt right at the correct angle for...."

"Hey," Tim yells, "You are referring to my wife, and I do not appreciate your lewd remarks! Get the hell away from our table, and leave my wife alone! If you ever touch my wife, I will slit your throats!"

"Julia, do you know these two guys?"

"No, I do not. I have seen them at the gym, but they have never approached Amanda or me."

"Gentlemen, I do not appreciate your gestures or your language. If

you insist on harassing my husband and me, I will have you arrested."
Julia pulls her police badge from her purse.

Immediately, the two guys leave the restaurant. The rest of the
dinner is quiet. Conversation between them has stopped. Julia knows
the encounter with those two guys has undone everything she and
Tim worked so hard to build. Hopefully, she can recover the feeling
with Tim, even if it means to get him 'laid' again.

The drive from the restaurant was quiet until Tim spoke up
disgruntled.

"Julia, I believe you when you say that you do not know those two
guys, but I am angry to hear that your workout routine encompasses
moves that place your ass into a manner suggesting 'come and get me
and stick it right in here'."

"Timothy Lillus I am surprised after all we have built in our
relationship the last few weeks, you think such things. I do not know
those guys nor any other male that happens to be in the gym when I
am there. I can't help what men may think of me and my body or
imagine I am suggesting with my body, but I can control what actions
I take with those type of remarks. No men have yet approached me, so
you have nothing to worry about."

AS SOON AS JULIA AND TIM ARRIVE AT THEIR HOME, JULIA DASHES TO THE
BATHROOM

"Julia, where are you going? We are not finished with this
conversation."

"Please, Tim, calm down. I wish to have a peaceful conversation
with you. There is no reason for you to be angry with me. I need to go
to the bathroom. I will be right out."

WHILE IN THE BATHROOM JULIA PLACES A CALL TO AMANDA SHORES

"Amanda, this is Julia. If you get this message, I need you to stop at my home. I feel that Tim is going to harm me. His jealous rage is mounting, because of two guys who made lewd remarks to me while we were having dinner. I am calling you from the bathroom, and I do not want Tim to hear me so I cannot give you too many details right now. Please hurry! I need you!"

Julia quietly walks from the bathroom to the bedroom where she slips on her red teddy and black fishnet stockings, hoping this outfit will snap Tim out of his fit of rage, encouraging him to have sex with her.

"Julia! Why are you wearing that? Are you trying to mock me out?"

"No, Tim, I put this on specifically for you. I know how much it turns you on and I was hoping that you wanted to take me to our bedroom so you could get 'laid'," as she reaches for his groin to press against his penis.

"Stop it!" exclaims Timothy. "I don't want to fuck you when you have had other men's dicks stuck into your pussy," as Timothy points to Julia's crotch.

"Oh, Timothy, for the love of God! Stop it!" exclaims Julia.

"I do not believe it or you! The more I think of it, the more I am sure you are having an affair and giving your pussy for the asking to those guys…or even other men! I will not put up with it anymore. How could you not know they were watching your ass in your provocative gyrations? I am sure you loved it. I have had it!" Tim exclaims as he pulls something out of the coffee table drawer.

"Tim, you just told me that you believed me when I told you I did not know those two guys and they have never approached me at the gym. I never saw them watching me. They are always with the teenage girls. They were just pumping their ego at the restaurant because you were there with me. You know, it is a guy thing!"

"Yeah, sure, Julia, I was thinking back on that hot sex we had the other night! You were pretty versed in your 'moves' and how to satisfy yourself and me. That doesn't come without practice and lots of it," yells Tim.

"Timothy Lillus! My 'moves', as you say, are not the result of practice with other men. The 'moves' result in knowing how to please my husband satisfactorily. You know we have had plenty of hot sex sessions, as you call them. Those were OUR practice, Tim! I love you with all my heart! Timothy, what will it take for me to convince you that I love you?" yells Julia. "I wish you would continue your counseling for your sickness. I want to help you get through this, and I know that together we can."

"Please, Tim, please don't hurt me! I am your wife! Please, don't do this!" exclaims Julia with tears running down her cheeks.

Tim moves towards Julia and grabs her arm sternly.

"Tim, you are hurting me! You are hurting my arm. Please...let...let..let go of my throat," Julia screams. "No, no, please no. Tim, I love you!"

In the next moment, Julia feels a warmth coming from her side, her shoulder, and then in her stomach just as the pain starts to register in her brain. Julia's blood oozes from the knife wounds on her body inflicted with the steak knife that Timothy thrust into her.

"Julia, you untrustworthy slut!" yells Tim.

"Oh, Tim, why?" asks Julia as her voice fads away.

Julia falls to the floor lifeless as her tears continue to flow onto the floor.

Timothy looks down at his wife lying on the floor and wonders for a short minute whether he did the right thing. He questions, "Why?"

AMANDA LISTENS TO JULIA'S MESSAGE. SHE RUSHES OVER TO THE LILLUS' S
HOME AS FAST AS SHE CAN

———

Suddenly, there is a knock at the door.

"Timothy Lillus this is Amanda Shores. Let me in! You better not
be hurting Julia! She is your wife!"

"Timothy Lillus if you do not open this door immediately, I will
have no choice but to kick it open."

Amanda, being an ex-cop, knows how to break through a door and
with her consistent workout routines, has the strength to do it.
Amanda kicks the door open with brute force. She sees Timothy
Lillus in the middle of the living room with a knife in hand and Julia
slumped to the floor with her blood pouring out over the rug and
tears from her eyes, pooling under her head.

"Timothy, what have you done to Julia?" as she rushes over to him
and Julia's lifeless body. "….Oh...oh...look at all of this blood!" Amanda
exclaims. "Oh, and her tears! It is so unfortunate. I am so sorry, Julia."

"Timothy, how could you have killed Julia, your wife? She loved
you dearly! You are a real bastard! Don't you see her tears of sorrow? I
am calling an ambulance."

———

BEFORE AMANDA CAN STEP AWAY FROM TIM, HE GRABS HER BY THE ARM,
AND THRUSTS HIS KNIFE IN HER THROAT AND THEN INTO HER CHEST.
IMMEDIATELY, AMANDA FALLS TO THE FLOOR, DEAD, AS HER BLOOD FLOWS
OUT OF THE STAB WOUNDS

———

Timothy is a very jealous man, but not a killer, at least until tonight.
Everything happened so fast that he did not have time to think. If
Timothy couldn't have Julia all to himself, then no one could have her.

He kept thinking why she had to have an affair or affairs. Wasn't he good enough, he pondered? No, it wasn't that, not that at all. She just flaunted her body wherever she went. It was a game. The slut! Then he thought about what he and Julia did a few weeks ago. He got laid, and it felt good. He would never feel that feeling again. He couldn't trust another woman. Not now, not ever!

Timothy has to sit down for a while and let what he did sink in. Muttering to himself, "I just wanted to give Julia what she had coming to her and then that bitch Amanda had to interfere. It is very complicated now. I need to dispose of two bodies so no one can find them."

The first thing that Timothy does is to strip Julia's teddy and stockings off of her body. They are special to him; lots of hot sex in those. But, of course, he will need to wash them right away to get the blood out. He doesn't want to strip Amanda's clothes off her; after all, she is nothing to him. She is just another slut, and her nude body will do nothing for him. Timothy, then, begins to wrap each one of them in a lawn and leaf bag. He has to stop the blood from oozing all over his floor. Timothy takes one last look at Julia's nude body and remembers just weeks ago how they had hot sex. He thinks about how he is the last man to see her pussy.

"Take that you bastards! I get the prize!" Timothy exclaims as if there is a contest to see who will be the last one to see Julia in the nude. He immediately erases these thoughts from his head. It hurts too much to remember all the intimate moments with Julia. He pushes Julia's body into the leaf bag and closes it with duck tape while wrapping the bagged body with turns of tape to get the air out. Tim proceeds to prepare another leaf bag in the same fashion for Amanda's body. He cleans the blood from the floor, and the rug with some extra bed sheets and then stashes them into a plastic bag and secures the bag to Amanda's bag. Timothy puts the steak knife, used to kill Julia and Amanda, in the dishwasher. "No one will find the murder weapon," thinks Timothy.

"It will just blend itself into the ordinary steak knife drawer where it was yesterday before I put it into the coffee table drawer." Timothy scours the living room to be sure there is no leftover blood anywhere, especially on the rug. It is challenging to clean the rug, but seeing it has some light pink coloring in the design, any slight leftover blood will blend into the other colors in the carpet.

With all of the nervousness that Timothy is feeling at the moment, he continues to mutter to himself. "I just knew that old car in the backyard would become useful someday. Besides, I can finally get it out of my yard. I will have to be careful, though, because the front doors no longer latch properly and I do not want the bodies to fall out of the car as I am sinking it into the creek. I cannot put the bodies in the trunk because that trunk lid will not stay down or even latch."

Timothy carefully places Amanda's body in the back seat of the old car. He puts Julia's body in the passenger seat. As the passenger door is closed, duct tape is wrapped around the frame so that the door will not open by itself. He makes sure that all of the windows are open so that the car will surely sink. Tim waits until dark, and then he quietly goes out to the car and starts its engine. Timothy is surprised it started the first time because it had been over a year since he drove it from his driveway to the backyard. Slowly, but deliberately he drives the car to the creek. Timothy stops the engine at the bank and puts the gear of the transmission into neutral. With the help of the decline of the terrain at the bank, he pushes the car out into the creek. There is a strong current because it is a part of the river, and used as a natural basin for excess water flow, after a heavy rain. The current should drag the car to the middle of the creek where it is the deepest.

Timothy knows there will be no suspicion of foul play, at least for a couple of weeks, because Julia had notified the Department that she and Amanda were going out on a cruise.

"At least I have some time to think of an alibi when they don't come back," muttered Timothy. "Well, I am all cleaned up. I guess I will go see a movie."

LOOKING FOR JULIA

About a week later as Timothy Lillus is relaxing in his living room watching a soap opera, his phone rings.

"Hello. Is this Timothy Lillus?"

"Yes, it is."

"This is Officer Peltz from the Harford Police Department."

"Oh, yes, how are you, Officer Peltz?"

"I am doing all right. I called because Julia, your wife, had told us that she was going on a cruise a week ago, but she hasn't shown up for work. I thought that she would be back by now."

"Well, to tell you the truth Officer Peltz, she wired a message to me stating that she would not be back for another week. Julia and the other passengers had to dock in the Bahamas to wait out a possible hurricane zeroing in their path."

"Oh, how lucky she is."

"Yeah, now I wished that I could have gotten off work to go with her," Timothy replies.

"Let her know when she gets back; we have a whole desk full of

police reports for her to sort through. Tell her the vacation is over!"
Officer Peltz says in a jokingly sarcastic manner.

"OK, I will, Officer Peltz. Have a good day."

THE PHONE CALL FROM THE POLICE DEPARTMENT RATTLES TIMOTHY. HE IS
ABLE TO STALL OFFICER PELTZ FOR THE MOMENT, BUT HE HAS TO THINK
OF ANOTHER EXCUSE WHEN THEY CALL BACK, MISSING JULIA AT THE
POLICE STATION. THE CRUISE EXCUSE CAN ONLY LAST SO LONG

THE DISCOVERY

Meanwhile, back at the Harford Police Department, there is a new development.

"Chief Roland, dispatch just called and said there is a car surfacing in the creek down by the river."

"A what?"

"A car!"

"What the hell is a car doing in the creek?"

"Well, Chief, you need to get down there and see for yourself. They are getting ready to pull it out of the water."

As the car is pulled out of the water, Chief Roland notices that the car doors are open and a black sack or something is in the back seat.

"What the hell is that black sack in the back seat?" the Chief asks.

"It's not a sack. It is a lawn and leaf bag and...oh crap, there is a body in it!" exclaimes Officer Peltz as he cuts the bag open.

"Oh, shit," the Chief cries out. "Is the body recognizable?"

"It is a female, and by the looks the way she is dressed, she was at a gym sometime. I would say that her age is about mid '30s. Oh crap, she has been stabbed in the throat and her chest. It appears an instant death before she was put into the car," says Officer Peltz.

Chief Roland then asks, "Does the car look familiar to anyone?"

"Well, it is an old one. It appears to be a 1970 Ford Pinto; red," says another Officer at the scene.

"Doesn't Lillus up yonder have one of those parked in his backyard?" asks the Chief.

"Yeah, I think he does," says Officer Peltz.

"Timothy Lillus is not readily on my mind as a suspect. The woman, here, isn't his wife and besides, Julia is out on a cruise. Hell, even if she weren't on a cruise, and this body was Julia's, he would be a real insane jerk to kill off that beautiful wife of his," Chief Roland states.

"OK, we need to get the Coroner here to take the body for identification and I want the car looked over with a fine tooth comb for possible evidence of who may have done this," Chief Roland says while stepping into his patrol car.

THE CORONER HAS PICKED UP THE BODY AND PERFORMING THE AUTOPSY

The Coroner has just finished the autopsy when Chief Roland of the Harford Police Department enters.

"Well, Sam, what did you find from the autopsy?"

"You guys are pretty accurate. The woman is about 32 to 33 years of age. She has been stabbed in the throat and her chest. The stab to the throat was the lethal one. The funny thing is the weapon used looks as if it was an ordinary steak knife. I am surprised that it was strong enough to do such damage."

"Has she been raped, Sam?"

"No, not that I can tell. It does not appear that any of her clothes have been removed. There are no tears or rips in her genital area, so I do not suspect penetration. I don't think the motive for murder was to rape. We will be taking DNA samples from all parts of her body as usual."

"Such a loss for such a beautiful woman," Sam mumbles.

BACK AT THE OFFICE, CHIEF ROLAND TAKES A FEW PHONE CALLS

"Hey, can you put me through to the Chief? It is Sam, here, at the Coroner's Office."

"Sure, please hang on a second," answers the receptionist.

"Yes, Sam, this is Chief Roland."

"Do you remember the woman officer who used to work for the Palermo County Police Station? She retired a few years back. Remember her husband passed unexpectedly and left her with a huge fortune?"

"Yeah, yeah, oh what was her name? Hmm. Amanda, Amanda Shores, I believe," Chief Roland remembers.

"She is our murder victim," states Sam.

"Oh, hell, who would want to murder her? They couldn't get to her money by murdering her. It is all tied up in trusts, IRA's, etc.," says Chief Roland.

"And, oh, we found some human skin under her nails and it doesn't appear to be hers. I think that maybe she scratched whoever was stabbing her," Sam states.

"Chief, dispatch just called and said that they took a trip past Timothy Lillus's house and noted the old Pinto in the backyard was no longer there," announces the receptionist. "Hmm," says Chief Roland. "That is strange."

"Chief, Jeffrey's Auto Autopsy just called and said that they found some clumps of long black hair in the door casing of the Pinto and sent it over to Sam for analysis," states the receptionist.

"Hello, Sam?"

"Yes, this is Sam. "

"Chief Roland here, have you finished the analysis of the hair Jeffrey's Auto Autopsy sent you?"

"It doesn't belong to the body of the female that was found dead in the back seat, and being it is black in color..."

"That's right, Amanda is a blonde. So......another body? But where?" Chief Roland asks.

QUESTIONS

Timothy Lillus's phone rings while he is sitting in his living room watching another soap opera.

"Timothy, may I please speak to Julia?" Officer Peltz asks. "No, you can't because she is sick in bed. I think that she must have picked up some bug while on the cruise," Timothy responds.

"When she is feeling better, have her call the Department please, oh, and by the way, Chief Roland wants me to ask you about your old Ford Pinto. He was thinking that maybe you might be willing to sell it to his son who is just getting his learners permit," says Officer Peltz.

"Tell the Chief that I no longer have it. Julia said it was a real eyesore and that I needed to get it out of our yard. So, I had it towed to the junkyard while she was on the cruise so it would be a surprise to her when she came home. Unfortunately, she is too sick even to notice," Timothy states.

"OK, just relay the message to Julia to hurry up and get well."

"I will."

MORE PHONE CALLS TO AND FROM THE POLICE DEPARTMENT

"May I speak to Chief Roland, please?"

"Yes, Sam, this is Roland."

"The human skin found under the nails of our deceased woman does not match the DNA of anything on her body. It does not match the DNA of the black hair found either. Also, there was no penetration."

"Thank God the poor woman wasn't raped too," responds Chief Roland.

"These are all of the DNA sample reports I have for now."

"OK Sam, we have variables but have nothing to tie them together. Keep in touch and let me know if you find out anything further."

"Hello, is this George's Auto Recycling?" asks Chief Roland.

"Yes, it is. What can I do for you?"

"This is Police Chief Roland of the Harford Police Department. Did you take in any Ford Pinto cars; I would say early 70's and red in color, lately?"

"Chief what in the sam hill are you asking? I haven't seen one of those since dinosaurs roamed the earth," George remarks.

"Are you sure about that?" asks the Chief.

"Yup, I do inventory on every junker that comes in my door, daily, and we don't have any Ford Pinto's."

SOMETHING IS FISHY

Back at the Harford Police Department, Chief Roland calls an emergency meeting with Officers Peltz and Fritz.

"Peltz!"

"Yes, Chief."

"Can you and Officer Fritz come into my office?"

"We may have a problem here. Lillus's Ford Pinto is missing from his yard. We pulled the same or similar car from the creek. Lillus told us he had taken his Ford Pinto to the junkyard. I called the junkyard, and they don't have any Ford Pintos. We learned from Auto Autopsy there were clumps of black hair found on the door casing of the sunken car. So, what color is Timothy Lillus's wife's hair? Black or brunette," the Chief answers his own question along with officer Fritz.

"And, I haven't heard from Julia since she went on that cruise. What cruise line was it anyway?" asks the Chief.

"Small Island Cruise Lines, I believe. At least that is what Timothy told me," says Officer Peltz.

"Julia would have touched base with us, sick or not. She always has," responds the Chief.

"Something does not add up...or does it? And, what about Amanda? How does she fit into this picture? And, if the hair belongs to Julia, then where is she?" the Chief ponders.

"Peltz, get a hold of the Small Island Cruise Lines and tell them that you have official business and want to know if a Mrs. Julia Lillus was registered as a guest on any of their cruises in the last two weeks. Fritz, I want you to go to Julia's locker and look to see if she has a hairbrush and get a strand of hair from it. Take it over to the Coroner's Office for DNA testing," orders Chief Roland.

TESTING, TESTING

J effrey's Auto Autopsy has made an important discovery.

"Chief Roland! This is Jeff at Jeffrey's Auto Autopsy. We found some blood stains on the passenger side seat cushion. We sent it over to the Coroner's Office."

"Great! We will get back to you if we need more. By the way, did you find any identifying papers in the glove box?" asks Chief Roland.

"No, it was clean just like the missing license plates and registration sticker on the windshield. No traces of ownership anywhere. I can do a trace on the vehicle registration number to find proof of ownership," says Jeff.

"I have a feeling I will not need that. Thanks," Chief Roland responds.

SAM, THE CORONER, HAS SAD NEWS

"Hello, Chief?"

"Yes."

"You need to come over here and see me immediately!" exclaims Sam.

"I am on my way."

"Sam, what's up? What did you find?"

"I did a DNA test on the clumps of black hair found on the door casing and matched it with Julia's strands of hair Officer Fritz brought to me. Chief, they are a direct match. The hair is Julia's," says Sam.

"And that is not all. The blood found on the passenger side of the front seat does not match the blood on the back seat or the woman, Amanda, who laid dead in the car. It appears that you have another body to find, Chief."

"I am afraid I know who the other body is. The poor sweet woman," replies Chief Roland.

"Julia," says Sam sadly.

MURDER

J ulia is presumed dead!

"Peltz, get a dive team out here and have them start dredging the creek. Being that the car doors were open and with the swift current of the river, the other body may have been dragged downstream. Fritz, it looks more and more like Lillus did something to his wife," says the Chief.

"You mean murder?" asks Officer Fritz.

"The hair is a match, and the car is very suspect of being Timothy Lillus's. Yes, it appears that you may be correct. The only other piece of evidence that would give us proof, is matching the blood found on the car seat to Julia's," says Chief Roland.

"We have enough to get a search warrant. We need to find traces of Julia's blood in Timothy Lillus's house, if any. I am going to send you and Peltz over to Lillus's house with the warrant. Search every square inch if you have to. I suspect that Julia's blood will turn up somewhere over there. If you do not happen to find any blood, make an excuse to go to the bathroom while at the house and grab Julia's toothbrush. The lab may be able to get DNA samples from that. You know the drill, Fritz. Be careful of Timothy and be sure to put all the samples you find, including the toothbrush, in a plastic bag to ensure that there is no contamination. I want to be sure Lillus killed Julia. That bastard!" exclaims Chief Roland.

"Right on, Chief, not a problem. We will get on it right away. Peltz, get the car. We have a warrant to serve," states Officer Fritz.

THE WARRANT

Officers Peltz and Fritz pull up in front of Timothy Lillus's House.

"Bobbie, I will try to keep Lillus busy in conversation while you look for samples. Be sure to grab Julia's toothbrush as well. We need concrete evidence to arrest Timothy for the murders."

"Timothy Lillus, let us in! The Harford Police Department is demanding that you let us in! We have a warrant."

"What is this all about?" questions Timothy.

"I am Officer Peltz, and this is Officer Fritz. We have a warrant to search your house."

"Why? I haven't done anything wrong."

"Where is your wife, Julia?"

"She went to her mother's house in Terryville to get some rest. She has had the flu. She must have picked it up while on the cruise," Timothy gestures.

"Why are you searching my house?"

"There was a body found in the creek, and we have reason to

believe that you know something about it," Officer Fritz sternly replies.

"A body! In the creek? Why...why would you suspect I had anything to do with it? I don't like the creek. I hate the water."

While Officer Peltz and Timothy are in conversation, Officer Fritz is searching the living room. As the interview is ending, Officer Fritz speaks up.

"Hey Peltz, take a look at this curled piece of rug under the chair. The color does not match the rest of the pattern of the rug, and there is a slight pink tint to it that doesn't seem to match."

"You're right, Fritz."

She reaches down a little further under the chair and sees a small clump of dark red, almost brown residue, on the rug. It was about the size of a small cake crumb and has a few strands of hair that are 'glued' within it, and they are black in color. Fritz lifts the 'crumb' and places it in a plastic bag.

"I spilled my wine there yesterday. How clumsy of me, I tried to clean the stain, but you know how hard it is to get red wine stains out of a rug," Timothy states.

Peltz progresses, with Timothy accompanying, to the bedroom to search for more clues as to Julia's absence.

"Timothy, I need to use your bathroom," yells Bobbie who was still in the living room.

"Sure, it is the second door on the right as you go down the hall," replies Timothy.

BOBBIE SEES JULIA'S TOOTHBRUSH LYING ON THE BATHROOM SINK COUNTER AND SEIZES IT PLACING IT INTO ANOTHER PLASTIC BAG. SHE CAN'T HELP TO NOTICE A RED TEDDY NIGHTWEAR OUTFIT HANGING ON THE SHOWER CURTAIN ROD, EVIDENTLY TO DRY FROM WASHING IT. THE TEDDY HAD A HOLE IN THE BODICE. BOBBIE THOUGHT IT STRANGE. SHE KNOWS JULIA ENOUGH THAT SHE WAS NOT ONE TO KEEP, LET ALONE, WEAR WORN CLOTHING

JAMES ROBERTS

TIMOTHY

After the officers leave the house, Timothy starts pacing the floor and muttering. "They say they found a body. There is no way that they could pin it on me. I was very thorough in picking up the mess...except for that damn rug. How could I have missed it? They can test all they want, but they have nothing to match the blood. Surely the current in the river washed away all of the blood that was on the car seats. Why didn't that car sink into the river?"

"They will never find the knife I used...ha..ha..because I am using it while I eat my steaks."

"I think the story of Julia visiting her mother was a great idea. They cannot check it out because I did not give them an address or even a phone number..ha..ha..because there isn't any. Julia's mother is dead and has been for a few years. I don't think that they will try to prove Julia's whereabouts. I need to keep my cool."

"Those Police Officers will probably be back. But still will not find anything. They can't trace my car. I could have taken it to a junkyard way across town, but I felt no need for that. There were no identifications whatsoever in the car. I took care of that. No, no, they will never be able to pin the murders on me. I was careful, yes I was...."

THE CORONER

S am, the Coroner, has completed more DNA testing and has found impressive results.

"Chief Roland, I am afraid that I have bad news to tell you involving the suspect."

"What is it, Sam?"

"Well, the clump of black hair found on the door casing of the car matches the strands of hair that Officer Fritz brought to me that were 'glued' to that clump of residue found on Timothy Lillus's rug. The DNA matches. And, that clump of residue is certainly dried blood. It just so happens that it matches the blood found on the passenger side of the front seat of the car. I also tested the DNA found on Julia's toothbrush with the blood samples on the car seat, and they match."

"I will be damned!" exclaims Chief Roland.

"Sam, prepare a written report on your findings and get it to me in the morning."

"Are there more leads to the other body, er, I mean to Julia and where she might be?" Sam asks.

"No, not yet! That bastard murdered his wife! I'll be damned!" exclaims Chief Roland.

TIMOTHY IS QUESTIONED

Officers Peltz and Fritz travel to Timothy Lillus's house.

"Timothy Lillus, we are here to take you to the Station for further questioning. Please come with us," Officer Peltz says.

"Why do you have more questions? I told you everything I know the other day and Julia will be home tomorrow. I will have her report to the Station as soon as she arrives," states Timothy.

"Timothy, please, come with us."

"I didn't do anything! I don't have to come with you," says Timothy.

"Timothy, do we need to get a warrant or are you going to come with us peacefully?"

"OK, I will come with you to the Station, but I didn't do anything!"

OFFICERS PELTZ AND FRITZ ARRIVE AT THE POLICE STATION WITH
TIMOTHY

"Timothy Lillus, we have brought you to the station for questioning. I think that by now you know we have found dead bodies in the creek that were placed in a car which matches your Ford Pinto. I will not go into specifics, but it appears murder is involved," says Chief Roland.

"I...I..didn't do it!" exclaims Timothy.

"We are just questioning what you know at this time," says Chief Roland.

"Timothy, where were you on the night of the 8th, I believe that it was a Friday night?"

"I was home in my living room watching the television."

"Where is your old car, the Ford Pinto?"

"I told you. I took it to the junkyard. Julia was sick of looking at it in the yard."

"So, Tim, where is your wife, Julia?"

"I told the Officers the other day that she is at her mother's house resting because she had contracted flu while she was on the cruise."

"Timothy, I am getting the feeling that there is some confusion here," says Chief Roland.

"Why is that?" Timothy asks. "I am telling you everything I know."

"Well, Timothy, your Ford Pinto is not at the junkyard. We checked. The car submerged in the creek is a 1970 Red Ford Pinto. It is the exact description of your car, isn't it?"

"You must not have checked the junkyard that I took it too. I took it across town to a junkyard that would accept it."

"We checked Jerry's across town."

"That explains it because I took it to Georges Auto Recycling," says Timothy.

"Timothy, what cruise line did Julia take?"

"I told your office receptionist she went on a cruise with the Small Island Cruise Lines."

"Why was the rug in your living room stained pink, Timothy?"

"That is easy. As I told your Officers, while I was watching television that night, I spilled some wine over my chair. I tried to get the stain out, but you know how red wine stains. You can never get it completely out."

"Timothy, I am finished playing games with you!"

"I think that you murdered your wife, Julia, and sent her to the bottom of the creek in your Ford Pinto!" exclaims Chief Roland.

"No...no..I did not. I told you...."

"You told us lies, Timothy! Julia did not go on a cruise. We checked the cruise lines, and she was not a registered guest. I believe that she never went on a cruise."

"No..no...she did. Maybe I got the name of the cruise line mixed up..."

"We checked the junkyard that you said you took your old car to and they didn't have it. We checked on Julia's mother, and there is no such place, and Julia's mother died three years ago."

"No...no..I did not kill Julia...I..I..she will be home tomorrow," whimpers Timothy, sweating.

"Timothy Lillus, you and I both know that Julia will not be back tomorrow or anytime for that fact," retorts Chief Roland.

"Timothy, did you kill your wife?"

"No...no..I..I..," Timothy responds wringing his hands.

"Come on, Timothy, you are lying!"

"No...no I am not. I am confused...you got it all wrong..."

THE CONFESSION

Heated discussions continue at the Harford Police Department, and a startling realization appears.

"Timothy, I ask you. DID YOU KILL YOUR WIFE JULIA?" asks Chief Roland sternly.

"No..no..I am so confused..Julia..Julia…"

"Timothy Lillus, you might as well tell us that you killed Julia. We have all of the evidence that points to you murdering Julia and Amanda; placing their dead bodies in your red 1970 Ford Pinto; taking it to the creek hoping that it would sink in the river where the current would wash away your deed. You were sloppy! Julia's hair was found in the car. The blood stains on the seat matches Julia's DNA on her toothbrush. You say red wine on the rug? No, Timothy, that stain is Julia's blood. Lastly, Timothy, let me see your arm. Lift your sleeves. Where did you get those scratches? I'll bet that the skin fragments that we found under the fingernails of the victims you murdered are yours."

"No! No! I did not kill them! I don't even know an Amanda Shores."

"Come on, Timothy, how did you know I was referring to Amanda Shores as being a victim?" asks Chief Roland. "It will be much easier for you. Just confess!"

"No..no.......all right DAMN IT! Yes, I killed that BITCH! She was all over town fucking every guy that she met! I would watch her, and she would draw men to her like a magnet and they were the steel, and spreading her legs for them! She would go every Wednesday night and exercise with her workout at the gym. She would come home all sweaty, hair wet wearing Spandex® pants. She dressed very provocatively! Yeah, she was working out all right...working in and out on her back with her legs spread wide open!"

"Timothy, who was the other body in the car?"

"It was that slut, Amanda! She had seen me kill Julia, and I could not let her go knowing what I had done, so I killed her too! I wrapped those bitches in plastic bags and sunk them in the creek. It was the perfect setup. I had it all planned out......"

"Timothy Lillus, you have the right to remain silent. Anything you say can and will be used against you in the court of law," recites Chief Roland.

"Cuff him, Fritz."

"Timothy, you will be held in the Cloverville Jail until arrangements can be made to move you," says Chief Roland.

THE SENTENCE

T he court hearing in Harford is in session.

"All rise! The court of the late Mrs. Julia Lillus and Amanda Shores versus Timothy Lillus is now in session, the Honorable Judge Horton presiding," the bailiff announces.

"Are both the defendant and prosecution attorneys ready?" asks Judge Horton.

"Yes, we are, your Honor."

"Mr. Blount, how does the defendant plead?"

"The defendant pleads 'not guilty'."

"Mr. Bolton, you may start."

"I call Mr. Timothy Lillus to the stand."

"Timothy Lillus, do you solemnly swear to tell the truth and nothing but the truth so help you God?" asks the bailiff.

"Yes," answers Timothy.

"You may be seated."

"Mr. Lillus, what is your wife's name?"

"Julia, Julia Lillus."

"Mr. Lillus, on the night in question, where were you and where was your wife, Julia?"

"I was at home watching the television. Julia was out with her best friend, Amanda Shores. They were at the gym working out."

"Mr. Lillus, I understand that you tend to have a jealous nature specifically about your wife, Julia?"

"Well, Julia is a gorgeous woman, and I know any man would very much like to be with her. After all, I am. So, yes, I am a bit jealous and concerned she might get tangled up with other men. Not by her choice, you know."

"Mr. Lillus, you speak of your wife as if she is still with you. You do know that your wife is dead, don't you?"

"Yes…I do…I am just having a hard time not having her here with me."

"Mr. Lillus, while your wife Julia was at the gym working out, were you overly anxious for her return? Did you ever believe that she might run off with another man?"

"Yes, I worried about it all of the time."

"So, you did not trust your wife, Mr, Lillus?"

"Yes, I did. But as I said, I did not trust the men around her at the gym."

"Mr. Lillus, Julia, your wife, had a best friend who went to the gym with her?"

"Yes, Amanda Shores went to the gym with her."

"Mr. Lillus, back to that night, explain to me what events occurred when your wife, Julia, returned to your home after her workout."

"When my wife entered our house, she was sweating, and her hair was wet. She was wearing her Spandex® pants and a sports bra."

"Was this attire your wife was wearing typical to what she wore other times when she returned from the gym?"

"Yes, she said she wore that outfit specifically for me because it turned me on."

"Did that outfit turn you on, Mr. Lillus?"

"Yes, it certainly did."

"Because of the jealous nature that you say you have, did you question the whereabouts of your wife, Julia, the night of her disappearance?"

"Yes, I asked her how the workout was and questioned her whether any men had tried to hit on her."

"What was her response, Mr. Lillus?"

"She told me that her workout was great and that a couple of guys at the gym were stalking her."

"How did you react to that, Mr. Lillus?"

"I have to admit, I was not happy and became increasingly jealous."

"Mr. Lillus, what happened next?"

"Julia and I watched some television and later went to bed."

"Mr. Lillus, did you and your wife, Julia, share consensual intimacy? Did the jealousy you exhibit hamper your relationship in any way?"

"Julia and I regularly fucked, I mean had intercourse regularly," replies Timothy. "My jealousy did not hamper our relationship."

"Tell me what happened next?"

"After the stalking incident Julia told me about at the gym, I was concerned there might be more to it she was not sharing with me. She did come home very sweaty that night. She usually came home from the gym not sweating. So, yes, thoughts came across my mind that I might be sharing Julia with another man or men. I must say that, well, in bed, Julia was well versed in getting laid; increasingly so."

"Mr. Lillus, did you ever think of confronting Julia about your insecurities?"

"Yes, I did all the time."

"What was her response to you?"

"She would tell me that I was the only man she ever needed and wanted."

"Did you believe her, Mr. Lillus?"

"Well, I did until that night when we went out to dinner."

"Mr. Lillus, tell me about the night when you and Julia went out for dinner. What happened?"

"We were eating our dinner when these two guys came by our table and started making lewd remarks to Julia."

"What did they say or do?"

"They looked at Julia and said they had recognized her at the gym. They went on to remark about the provocative moves she was making with her workout, plus her outfit with Spandex® pants, well you know…"

"No, Mr. Lillus, I do not know. What did the two guys say to Julia?"

"They said she moved her body in such a manner, during her workouts, which situated her ass in a position that said, 'come and get it'."

"What did you have to say about that?"

"I asked Julia if she knew those guys and her answer was, she did not. She flashed her police badge at them and told them if they continued to assault her, she would have them arrested. The two guys left the restaurant."

"Mr. Lillus, did that incident bother you?"

"Your damned right it did! Julia and I got into an argument when we returned home."

"Mr. Lillus, was the argument you had with Julia involve any physical contact? Did you hit Julia or even…."

"Objection! The prosecution is leading my client. Insinuating that my client had struck his wife," the defense attorney Mr. Blount states.

"Objection sustained!" rules Judge Horton. "The prosecution will refrain from leading the defendant."

"Yes, your Honor," replies Mr. Bolton.

"Mr. Lillus, how long did your anger with the situation at the dinner last? How did Julia respond?"

"Julia tried to assure me that nothing was going on with those two guys or any other men. She provided me with 'hot and heavy sex' all night to prove to me that she was being truthful."

"Mr. Lillus, the next morning after what you called a night of 'hot and heavy sex', how did you feel? Were you still jealous of Julia? Did you believe her?"

"No, Julia performed sex that night like she had been rehearsing it many times. I was sure that she was playing out her sexual moves just as she did with those two guys and quite possibly, other men."

"Mr. Lillus, how angry did this make you?"

"I was quite angry and felt I needed to do something about it."

"Mr. Lillus, what did you do about it?"

"I thought about hiring a private detective to watch Julia."

"That is all the questions I have at the moment, Mr. Lillus."

"Mr. Lillus, you may step down," states Judge Horton.

"The prosecution calls Doctor Lewis Brandt to the stand," Mr. Bolton announces.

"Doctor Brandt, do you solemnly swear to tell the truth and nothing but the truth so help you God?" asks the bailiff.

"Yes," replies Doctor Brandt.

"Please be seated."

"Doctor Brandt, was at any time, Mr. Lillus, a patient of yours?"

"Yes, he was a patient of mine a few years past."

"Doctor Brandt, what did Mr. Lillus see you for?"

"Mr. Lillus was seeing me due to his wife describing to me that he had a huge jealousy problem and that it was affecting their relationship."

"Doctor Brandt, is it right for me to assume that Mr. Lillus's wife is the now deceased Julia Lillus?"

"Yes, she was Mr. Lillus's wife."

"Doctor Brandt, in your opinion, what was Mr. Lillus's diagnosis?"

"Mr. Timothy Lillus suffers from Pathological Jealousy or Othello's Syndrome."

"Doctor, describe to the court what Othello's Syndrome is."

"Othello's Syndrome is a very acute and serious form of jealousy which can result in adverse reactions by the individual suffering from it. A pathologically jealous individual establishes suspicions concerning the unfaithfulness of their partner. As soon as the doubts are established, the individual then turns to become possessed, and symptoms of the disorder begin to emerge. In the eyes of the morbidly jealous partner, the indicted 'significant other' is presumed guilty until evidence of innocence is found. The evidence, however, does not materialize, and brave efforts to demonstrate innocence or challenge guilt fail since irrational preoccupations in the mind of the suspicious partner cannot be refuted rationally. Moreover, the accused partner's rejection of infidelity could incite rage and violence. Under certain circumstances, the tolerant partner, who becomes plagued by the repeated interrogation and accusations of cheating, might provide false confessions which will provoke fury in the jealous individual."

"Doctor, in your own words, is it a possibility that a person inflicted with this form of jealousy could react so violently to cause death?"

"Yes, that person could be very capable of causing death if the affliction is not treated."

"One last question Doctor. Is Mr. Lillus still seeing you for medical help?"

"No, he is not. Most times the inflicted individual does not believe they have a problem. It appears to them that the one who is unfaithful or cannot be trusted is the one at fault."

"Thank you, Doctor Brandt. I have no further questions."

"Doctor Brandt you may step down from the stand," Judge Horton states.

"Are there any questions from the defense?" asks Judge Horton.

"Yes, the defense calls Mr. Timothy Lillus to the stand," replies attorney Blount.

"Mr. Lillus, let me remind you that you are still under oath," states the bailiff.

"Yes," responds Timothy.

"Please be seated."

"Timothy, is it true that you have a condition of Pathological Jealousy?"

"No, I believe that I do not."

"What do you attribute to your jealousy?"

"Well, I think that any man in this court would agree that if he has a beautiful wife, jealousy plays a part in the relationship. My wife Julia had often told me that she liked my jealous streak because it made her feel secure that I cared enough about her to be jealous."

"So, Mr. Lillus, you felt that your jealous nature was justified and that your wife, Julia, was not bothered about it. To her, it was a sense of security."

"Yes."

"Mr. Lillus, what do you feel happened to your wife, Julia?"

"I think that one of the men that showed up at dinner that night, who was remarking about her ass, was having an affair with her; the slut! I am sure he insisted that she ditch me, the jealous bastard!"

"So, Timothy, what do you think happened?"

"I believe that bastard couldn't deal with his jealousy and decided to get rid of her. That bastard took my wife from me!"

"I am being framed!"

"Mr. Lillus, explain to the court why you feel that you are being framed."

"I am being framed for the murder of Julia so that bastard can get away with it. I know it is one of those bastards in the restaurant, that night, who was remarking about her ass moving provocatively during her workouts!"

"Mr. Lillus, the Harford Police Department has completed tests which seem to prove that Julia was killed in your home; placed in your car and sunk in the creek. What is your take on this?"

"I am being framed! There are many old cars out there that match my car, and I did take my car to the junkyard regardless of what the police report stated. The blood they found in my house was Julia's. Julia sliced her hand in the very chair where they found her blood, while she was cutting up beans to can. The whole thing is bogus, and I would venture to say that those bastards utilized many various tactics to frame me. He was jealous and mad that I had Julia and he did not. That is my feeling."

"Mr. Lillus, one last question. Did you love your wife, Julia, and you would never harm her in any way?"

"Yes, I loved Julia, and I miss her so much," as tears flowed from

Timothy's eyes. "I may have been jealous, but I would never have hurt her. I wanted to protect her."

"Thank you, Mr. Lillus. It is all the questions that I have."

"Mr. Lillus, you may step down from the stand," states Judge Horton.

"The defense calls Doctor Lewis Brandt to the stand."

"Doctor Brandt, remember that you are still under oath," states the bailiff.

"Yes, I know."

"Please be seated."

"Doctor Brandt, how well do you know about this so-called affliction Pathological Jealousy?"

"I have studied quite extensively."

"In your estimation, Doctor, how many cases of this affliction have you diagnosed and treated?"

"Pathological Jealousy is quite common. I have teated approximately twenty of these patients."

"What is the treatment for this affliction, Doctor Brandt?"

"There is medication for it, but the side effects can cause adverse reactions to the patient to the extent of worsening the affliction. My recommendation is counseling for the patient. In this way, the patient can work through his or her affliction with the help of the counselor without medication."

"Doctor, what is the success rate of counseling to cure the affliction?"

"The affliction has been reduced to normalcy in most of the patients that I have treated. The affliction is not curable due to its origin coming from so-called 'crossed wires' in the patient's brain. It is the feeling that it is caused by a very recessive gene that, back in the old days, was blamed for insanity. I have been successful in bringing the patients jealousness to reasonable levels which most of the human population exhibits."

"Doctor, the records show that Mr. Lillus attended counseling for his jealous nature. Did you administer the counseling?"

"No, and I was not aware that Mr. Lillus had gone to counseling for his affliction."

"So, in your opinion, Doctor Brandt, could it be possible that through counseling Mr. Lillus could have been cured to the normalcy that you speak about?"

"Yes, I suppose that it could be possible."

"Would this normalcy that you speak of, Doctor Brandt, cause a person to inflict physical harm to another, such as murder?"

"If one was looking at the treated affliction, no, I do not feel normalcy would lead a person to inflict murder, but there are so many other factors that could."

"That is all Doctor Brandt. The defense rests," states attorney Blount.

"Doctor Brandt, you may step down from the stand," Judge Horton states.

"Does the prosecution have witnesses to question?" asks Judge Horton.

"No, your Honor, but the prosecution would once, again, like to question the defendant Mr. Timothy Lillus."

"This is highly unusual. Attorneys, please approach the bench," orders Judge Horton.

"Mr. Bolton, why do you feel that you need to question the defendant further?"

"Your Honor, due to the recent testimonies heard, I feel it important to bring into light dialogue from a document that could aid in the decision of this case. I want to read portions of the dialogue to the defendant."

"Mr. Blount, do you have any objection to the prosecution further questioning your client?"

"No your Honor, my client has answered all of the prosecuting attorney's questions; further questioning will not hamper his stance in this case."

"OK, Mr. Bolton, you may proceed, but keep your line of questioning to the facts."

"Yes your Honor."

"The prosecution calls Mr. Timothy Lillus to the stand."

"Mr. Lillus, let me remind you that you are still under oath," states the bailiff.

"Yes," responds Timothy.

"Please be seated."

"Mr. Lillus, the court has heard your testimony for this case, but I ask of you, how long did you go to counseling for the Pathological Jealousy affliction?"

"I would like first to say that I never believed I had, or have to this day, the affliction, but Julia suggested that I go to counseling regardless. I went to counseling for a month."

"Doctor Brandt has noted in his written testimony that the typical time frame to cure the affliction to normalcy is six months to a year."

"As I said, I do not have the Pathological Jealousy affliction. A month was good enough for Julia and me."

"Mr. Lillus, what would be your response if I told you that I have a witness with a sworn statement outlining what they had seen at the gym while Julia attended?"

"What do you mean?"

"Mr. Lillus, I have a document, here, which indicates someone had been with Julia at the gym and watched with detail every move of her workout. The witness accounted for everything right down to the descriptive nature of her workouts, such as you described the two guys in the restaurant had told you and Julia."

"I Knew it! I knew it!"

"What was that Mr. Lillus?"

"Nothing!"

"Be it known to the court that I have seen this document and have deemed it to be written by the witness and authentic," states Judge Horton.

Attorney Bolton opens the sealed envelope and prepares to read the document.

"I come to this gym regularly and continue to watch Julia Lillus perform her workout routine. I love seeing her move and the positions that she can put her body…"

Timothy Lillus starts to sweat, and his face starts to turn red.

"She sure has the body to perform those moves…"

Timothy Lillus squirms in his seat and sweat is now seen by all, running down his face as he quenches his fists.

"Every time I am at the gym, I just sit and watch Julia contort in ways…"

"That bitch! That bitch!" Timothy Lillus blurts out. "I knew those guys were telling the truth! Julia was provocatively performing her workouts! Those guys and, hell, who knows how many more, watched her ass as it circled begging to penetrate it! I knew she was having an affair! I knew she was cheating! That document proves it! I had to stop it….I had to stop that affair…no one was going to be fucking my wife except me! If I couldn't have her, then no one could, so I stabbed her…I killed that unfaithful bitch!"

Timothy slumps back into his chair realizing what he had just said in a fit of rage.

The courtroom roars in disbelief.

"Order! Order in this court" shouts Judge Horton as his gavel comes down hard on the wood block with a loud crack.

"Your Honor, I would like to finish reading this document to Mr. Lillus, if I may."

"Continue, Mr. Bolton."

"Every time I am at the gym, I just sit and watch Julia contort in ways I wish I could replicate. My best friend, Julia, is such a great inspiration to me. Every time we go to the gym and workout, she is more than willing to teach me her moves. It is a joy to know such a wonderful and talented person."

As Mr. Bolton continues to read the document, Timothy Lillus re-ignites his jealous rage; he is restrained by the court officials.

"Mr. Lillus, the document that I am reading is written by the late Amanda Shore, Julia's best friend, and is taken from her diary."

"How can that be? Oh, what the hell! I stabbed that bitch enough times so she would never talk," yelled Timothy.

"Court is dismissed and will reconvene at noon tomorrow," Judge Horton announces. "Please take Mr. Lillus to the court confinement area until court resumes tomorrow."

THE FOLLOWING DAY, COURT IS RESUMED

"Mr. Timothy Lillus, please rise. We have heard the testimonies of the witnesses and your testimony concerning the murders of your wife Mrs. Julia Lillus and Ms. Amanda Shores. At this time, I understand you are making a plea of temporary insanity. Mr. Lillus, I find it hard to believe, being you suffer from Pathological Jealousy, you failed to get help for it. The testimonies given prove a deliberate and well-planned execution of those two ladies and the means to hide the deed. Therefore I will not grant you temporary insanity. Timothy Lillus, the jury has found you guilty of the premeditated murders of Mrs. Julia Lillus and Ms. Amanda Shores. I sentence you to do your time in the Jackson City State Prison until the day that you die," says Judge Horton.

"The court is adjourned."

"Please rise," states the Bailiff.

OUTSIDE THE COURTHOUSE, THE TWO ATTORNEYS ARE IN CONVERSATION

"Hey, Bolton! That was a pretty swift move you pulled at the last minute."

"What do you mean, Blount?"

"Reading the excerpt from Amanda Shores' diary and wording as such to make it appear that the dialogue was coming from a male who was getting off watching Julia during her workout routines."

"I was reading it literally. I did not add any dialogue or remove any of it. I just cleverly read portions to get what I was looking for."

"And, Bolton, did you get what you wanted?"

"I sure did. I got Timothy Lillus's confession. We all knew he is guilty. We just needed proof. We needed him to say it."

"Bolton, you took a big risk, didn't you? How did you know your plan in reading Amanda Shores's, or should I say specific portions of Amanda's diary, would produce the results you needed?"

"I did quite a bit of research on 'Othello's Syndrome', which Timothy Lillus possesses. I learned that certain factors would trigger the affected person to act out and display outrage because the trigger challenged their jealousy. Timothy Lillus was outraged when he related to us the encounter he and Julia had at dinner when those two guys made sexually lewd remarks about a specific area of Julia's body. I decided it was a great time to keep the outrage 'fire' fanned. I gambled I would get a confession from Timothy Lillus, so I crafted the dialogue from Amanda Shores' diary to make it sound like a male was watching Julia during her workouts. The jealousy Timothy had, heightened to a level he could not handle. He wanted it to end, so for it to end, he needed to stop the triggers. The triggers that had to end was the court proceedings, and they did when he confessed."

"Very clever, Bolton, but how were you able to play this out in the proper order? What if Timothy Lillus told his story about the dinner at a different time during the proceedings? How did you know?"

"I didn't, Blount. But I was 'armed' just in case."

"Genius, Bolton, just genius!"

JACKSON CITY PRISON

The prisoner bus pulls up in front of the Jackson City Prison and Timothy Lillus is escorted to reception.

"Mr. Timothy Lillus?"

"Yes."

"Please give me all of the personal items in your pockets and change into these clothes. These clothes are what you will be wearing during your stay at this prison. Larry, please escort Mr. Lillus to the changing room," says the intake officer.

"Here are the schedules you will follow daily. Morning rise will be 7:00 am and breakfast at 7:30 am. At 8:30 am you will go out to the courtyard for exercise drills, weather permitting, and fresh air. From 10:30 am to noon, you will return to your cell."

"I suggest that you get some books from the library to pass the time."

"At noon you will take lunch in the cafeteria. You will have until 1:00 pm for lunch before you return to your cell. At 3:00 pm you will go back out to the courtyard. Dinner will be served at 5:00 pm in the cafeteria. To finish the day, you will go back to your cell and lights out at 9:00 pm," the guard states.

"We are the biggest county prison in the state and have over five hundred inmates so you will be sharing your cell. You do not have the option of picking the inmate you share a cell, so make it work."

"Follow me. Open B102," orders the guard.

"This is your cell, and this is Mr. John Bailey."

"Close B102," the guard once again orders.

INTRODUCTIONS

Timothy quickly looks over the cell and then stares blankly at his cellmate.

"I just learned your name. My name is Timothy Lillus. You can call me Tim."

"Why are you here?" asks John.

"I killed my wife. I found out that she was fucking every guy in town she could allure."

"I'll call you 'killer', then," John retorts.

"How long you in for, 'killer'?"

"Until I die. Life imprisonment!"

"And you, John?"

"They got it through their heads that I assaulted a student attending the elementary school where I was a music teacher."

"This child grabbed at my crotch while I was giving a piano lesson to her. I grabbed her hand and pushed it away. My hand slipped and went under her skirt. Later, she said that I placed my hand between her legs. The whole thing was a trumped-up thing," remarks John.

"They gave me fifteen years and branded me as a pedophile. Hell, they might as well have given me life!"

"John, are you a pedophile?" asks Timothy.

There is no reply to that question.

THE SUGGESTION

J ohn Bailey and Timothy Lillus reluctantly get along with each other. Neither trusts the other.

"Look, it appears you and I will have to get along with each other. It is going to take some work, though," says Timothy. "I will let you in on a little secret that just might get us out of here sooner."

"Oh no," says John. "We can't break out of here. How in the hell…"

"Listen, when I was eighteen years old, I joined a contracting outfit that ran all of the steam and drainage piping throughout this joint. I know how to get around behind these walls; where the piping is run. I am a pipe fitter by trade," says Timothy. "Knowing what I know of the construction of this building will give us a great advantage."

"What are you suggesting, 'killer'?"

"We break through the wall and find the steam pipes. Below those steam pipes is the large drainage pipe that runs the entire length of the prison. The drainage pipe is used for water run-off from the roof when it rains. It is thirty inches in diameter. We can slide through the drainage pipe to the central city sewer system. From there we can route to a distant manhole and then we are free," says Timothy.

"Whoa there, 'killer'. How do we get into the drainage piping and once we get out where do we go and...?"

"I will give more instructions later, but I can tell you we are going to Canada via the Niagara River," says Timothy.

"Yeah, sure, we have no tools and look at me. Do I look like I could fit into a drain pipe?" John says sarcastically.

"Well, John, I have a suggestion. Get your fat ass out in the courtyard and burn off that fat! Besides, the drain pipe is thirty inches in diameter. You will fit, or you won't go!" exclaims Timothy.

THE PLAN DETAILS

John Bailey reluctantly listens to Timothy's plan. He does not like it, but he sure as hell doesn't want to stay in prison.

"OK, 'killer', I am with you. Now, spell out the details of how we make this escape," says John.

"We will need to break into this wall, here. Once in, we will need to climb down to the drainage pipe. There is a clean-out tee about fifty feet down from this cell. And as I said, we crawl through to a manhole and flee to Canada."

"Canada? How the hell do we get there?" asks John.

"We travel to the border via the railroad tracks and make our way to Niagara Falls. We will then travel the Niagara River into Canada," explains Timothy.

"What the hell! How do we get into Canada via the river? Over the falls in a barrel?" John asks.

"I'll explain that later, John."

"OK, OK, let's back up a bit. How do we break through the wall and even more importantly, the drainage pipe with no tools, let alone someone seeing or hearing us?" John asks inquisitively.

"We will get the needed tools from the infirmary, but meanwhile we have these to break through the wall."

"Nail clippers? 'Killer', you are whacked. No wonder your wife sold, oh, I mean gave her sweet little pussy to other men," John jokingly spouts.

"Listen, you big pussy grabbing prick! You say that one more time and I will be the only one of the two of us who leaves this shit hole alive! I have no problem killing you. I can slit your throat with these nail clippers. Want me to show you? I have become a pro at it lately," Timothy brags.

"No need to demonstrate with those nail clippers. I believe you. Soooory, 'killer'."

"These walls are made with concrete blocks and held together with mortar. We will work the mortar out around two blocks with our nail clippers so that we can remove them and squeeze through. There are steel reinforcing bars the other side of the blocks that we will need to cut. Once we get through the wall and get to the drainage pipe, we find the clean-out tee, remove the bolts to the cap flange and crawl in."

"You are whacked, 'killer'. I suppose that the guards will plug their ears and close their eyes while we are doing it," states John.

"We will have to do this in shifts. Notice, with this mirror, you can see from one end of the cell block to the other. One of us will work while the other places the mirror between these bars and looks out for the patrolling guard. We will switch places every half hour," says Timothy.

"I'll be damned!" exclaims John.

"We will work at night after 9:00 pm and be ready to hop into bed when guard patrol is run," states Timothy.

"We only remove two concrete blocks?" asks John. "I do not think I can fit through."

"John, the courtyard; exercise!"

"We will have to remove the two blocks from the wall behind this sink. We will need to remove these screws through the sink from the wall and replace them each time, along with the two concrete blocks."

"Well, how the he......?"

"Hang on, John, I will get to that shortly," Timothy says.

"To break through the steel reinforcing bars on the other side of the concrete blocks; there is a trick to it. We heat the steel bars to red-hot color. Then immediately cool them with ice and 'bam' kick them in half," says Timothy.

"Now, you are starting to worry me, 'killer'. Those bars won't break as you describe. They are solid steel."

"Oh yes they will, and you will only hear a small 'snap'. See, the reinforcing bars are made of low carbon cheap steel. By heating and rapid cooling the steel becomes brittle, and with just a kick they will snap."

"Whoa, 'killer', slow down a little. How do we heat those reinforcing bars?" asks John.

"See that light up there?"

"Yes."

"Electricity is all we need with a little wire. That and a thunderstorm to mask the dimming of the lights which will occur. The drainage pipe will need to be empty before we remove the bolts from the flange to the clean-out tee. We will need to wait for a clear day after the storm for the drain pipe to empty."

"So, how do we remove the bolts in the drainage pipe without making noise?" asks John.

"That is where we are blessed. This cell block is on the ground floor level, and the drainage pipe is down below us out of the earshot of the guards."

"Once we get through the wall and one of us is on the lookout, how do we notify the other who is working the bolts to the drainage pipe flange when a guard is doing his patrol?" asks John.

"We will hang a rag just outside the concrete block opening. When a patrol guard is on his way to our cell, the person watching for him will slide the rag to the inside of the opening alerting the other. All you have to do is look for the rag slung into the opening," says Timothy.

"I also wish to have a ruckus started with the other inmates to create noise and keep the guards busy."

"How we going to do that?" asks John.

"You will, you overgrown pedophile. You will cause the ruckus," Timothy gestures.

THE CONFRONTATION

T imothy and John's criminal backgrounds start to clash after the remark that Timothy just made to John.

"Stop glorifying me!" John muses.

"I am not! I loathe anything or anyone who harms children. I only put up with you because I need you for the escape! I am placing my bets that you will not survive in the outside world as a child molester. You wouldn't dare take your chances of getting yourself back in here because you say that you are in here by false accusations, didn't you John?" asks Timothy sarcastically.

"Looks to me John you are just going to have to keep it in your pants, and your hands out of zippers and panties for the rest of your life. You are disgusting!"

"Whoa, 'killer', you should talk! Jeesh, killing your wife? You should be glad that your wife was sexually active! What was the matter, 'killer'? She couldn't get any at home, or you couldn't keep it up long enough to satisfy her?"

"I already told you, prick, do not talk about my wife that way!" Timothy yells.

"You mean your once upon a wife, don't you, 'killer'?"

"Look I had a knife and stabbed her a couple of times. It took that bitch a long time to die!" Timothy speaks infuriated.

"It won't take long for you to die, though. Do you know why? I will cut your cock off. Did you know there are a lot of blood vessels down there, you prick? You will bleed to death in a flash!"

"So don't tempt me, John! At least I own up to my crimes," Timothy exclaims sternly.

"You, John, on the other hand, hide behind the 'I am holier than though because I was a school teacher.' Sexually assaulting children; you are a disgrace! I don't know why I bother to bring you along with the escape."

"We do have at least one thing in common, 'killer'."

"Yeah, John, I do not believe we have anything in common."

"We do. We have both fucked women, haven't we? You must have fucked your wife at least once, Timothy?"

"Shut the fuck up, you pussy grabber…shut the fuck up!"

THE WORKINGS

T imothy continues to lay out the plans for the escape to John.

"I am a diabetic, and I have to go to the infirmary from time to time to have my sugar levels checked. It is during those times I will be working to get the tools we need," says Timothy.

"How are you going to do that?" John asks.

"I will be able to get a cast of the key to the infirmary. The tools we need are in there."

"Sure, you are just going to walk in there and get a key made and then walk out with the tools? 'Killer', you are not making a hell of a lot of sense."

"Well, the first thing that I have to do is get friendly with the nurse to get her to lower her guard and trust me. It will take some time, but we need that time to get through the wall. Once I gain the trust of the nurse, she will not be so watchful of me."

"We will need to get some caulk from the machine shop for me to make the mold of the infirmary key. You, John, are the one who is going to get the tools we need from the infirmary."

"Wait a minute!" exclaims John. "Why me? I don't like this."

"John, you make the rounds for dispensing books to the other inmates, and your route goes right past the infirmary."

"Here is the plan. It just so happens that my appointment for testing is about the time for your library rounds. The library is next to the infirmary, right John?"

"Yes, it is."

"I will keep the nurse occupied while you unlock the door and get the tools we need. The last time I was in for testing, a guard came in and grabbed some tools from the cabinet next to the barred window. I noticed that they don't lock the cabinet door."

"But what about the guards?"

"It just so happens your route starts at 10:00 am, and you will be right in the area of the infirmary at about 10:30 am. My appointment is at 10:30 am, and there is a fifteen minute period when the guard's shift changes. That would bring it to 10:45 am. During that brief moment, the guards are down the hall and around the corner. There are no cameras in front of the infirmary door. I do not know why there are no cameras in the hall leading to the entrance of the infirmary. It is probably because the infirmary door is always locked, even when an inmate is visiting the nurse. You will only have approximately five minutes to unlock the door, grab the tools and get back out and lock the door. Once out of the infirmary you continue to go down the hall to the next corner."

"It just so happens before you get to the door of the infirmary and before you turn the corner some books fall off of your cart. This stalling tactic will appear to the guards on camera and won't alarm them. You know, you have to pick up the books, don't you? They won't be alarmed. You will put the tools in the pages of a book. By the time you get to our cell, I will be back, and you will pass me a couple of books with the tools."

John asks, "How did you devise this plan with so much precision?"

"John, what do you do with your time while here? I look around and observe while taking mental notes," says Timothy.

"I do not think that I can get the tools into a book without them showing," John says.

"The tools we will need are an adjustable wrench and a flat bladed screwdriver. Make sure to get the loose leaf book of the moon landing pictures for me. I want to brush up on the moon landings," Timothy says jokingly.

"Slide the tools inside the slots of the cover. I will take care of getting the baby oil."

"Baby oil?" asks John.

"Yeah, we will need to spread baby oil all over our bodies to help us slide through the drainage pipe."

"Yuck," says John

"Oh, come now, John, I am sure that you are very familiar with baby oil," Timothy sarcastically remarks.

RONNIE

Timothy uses his charm with the nurse in the infirmary. She reminds him of Julia.

———

"Your name?" asks Ronnie.

"Timothy Lillus, ma'am."

"You are here for a blood test?"

"Yes ma'am."

"How long have you had diabetes, Mr. Lillus?"

"Over ten years ma'am."

"Your sugar levels appear to be normal. I will see you next week at the same time at 10:30 am?"

"Yes ma'am."

———

A WEEK PASSES, AND TIMOTHY IS ONCE AGAIN VISITING THE INFIRMARY

———

"Good morning, Mr. Lillus," says Ronnie.

"Please, call me Tim. After all, I have been seeing you for a couple of weeks."

"Yes, you have."

"Do you mind me calling you Ronnie? That is your name isn't it?"

"Yes, that is my name."

"Ronnie, you know, I have been falsely accused of murdering my wife. My lawyer has told me they have found the guy who killed her. They are working to get me out of here."

"That is good to hear, Tim."

"You know, Ronnie, you remind me so much of my wife. She had long brunette hair and about as tall as you. She was slender like you and had slightly oval eyes and little dimples on her cheeks."

"Tim, she must have been beautiful. What was her name?"

"Julia, Julia Lillus."

"Oh, yes, I remember reading about that in the newspapers. You say you have been found innocent? The news media appears to have painted a very tightly shut case against you with all of the evidence the local Police Department has given."

"Yeah, it is sickening! The news media always paints a bad picture. But they have it all wrong, and I will be out of here soon. You see, my wife was having an affair and it turns out the guy she was having an affair with actually murdered her and her best friend."

"Oh, Tim, I am so sorry. You must be heartbroken. I am sure you loved your wife even though she was having an affair? Did you know that she was having an affair?"

"I pretty much guessed it from the beginning and, yes, I loved her, and it hurts."

"So, Tim, what are you going to do when you are released?"

"I don't know; I will have to think on it."

"Tim, I have another appointment. I will see you again, next week."

"OK, bye, Ronnie."

THE FOURTH WEEK ROLLS AROUND

"Wow, Ronnie, it sure is a pleasant surprise seeing you this week!"

"Why is that Tim?"

"The clothes you are wearing…."

"What's the matter Tim, haven't you seen a woman in Spandex® pants before?"

"Yes, as a matter of fact, I have. Julia, my wife, wore those when she went to workout. The only difference to what I see now is that you are not wearing the matching sports bra like Julia used to wear."

"Tim, I have a sports bra on under my shirt. I am going to the gym after work."

"Tim, it appears that you are quite excited," Ronnie states as she looks down at his groin.

"Yeah, Ronnie, the outfit that Julia wore was exciting for me and seeing you in a similar outfit just crushes me."

"Hey Ronnie, once I get out, do you think that we could have dinner together sometime?"

"I think that might be possible. Excuse me, Tim, I need to get the bottle of baby oil for your dry skin."

"OK, I will be waiting for your return."

RONNIE LEAVES HER KEYS ON THE COUNTER NEXT TO TIMOTHY. HE TAKES THE CAULK OUT FROM UNDER HIS SHOE. IT HAS HARDENED ENOUGH TO BE MOLDED LIKE CLAY. IMMEDIATELY, HE SINKS THE INFIRMARY DOOR KEY INTO THE CAULK; THEN PUTS THE MOLD INTO HIS POCKET

"Here is your baby oil Tim. I will give you this prescription slip to show the guard."

"Thank you so much, Ronnie. I will see you in a few weeks, hopefully having dinner. By the way, you have beautiful blue eyes, Ronnie."

"Oh, thank you Tim. Take care."

THE GUARD IS SO FOCUSED ON TIMOTHY'S BOTTLE OF BABY OIL AND THE PRESCRIPTION SLIP, HE FORGETS TO CHECK THE POCKETS OF TIMOTHY'S PRISON SUIT

"I guess my plans work even without my interaction. John, he never checked my pockets. Can you believe it?" asks Timothy.

"Yeah, what did you have to do to get that nurse busy enough not to see you take her keys, 'killer'?"

"I dazed her with my charm, and she let her guard down. I wish I didn't have to leave this place. I have grown quite fond of her."

"Yeah, but what could you do with her in here? You couldn't even touch her. What good is that?"

"That's what you think, John. There are ways."

"By the way, will we be able to break those concrete blocks out of the wall soon?"

"Yup, 'killer', we will."

THE MACHINE SHOP

Each day, there is time for the inmates to make things in the machine shop. Most of the items are for county or state use such as license plates, street signs, and road markers. Occasionally they can make a few personal things to help against onset boredom.

"Today, John, we make the key. I will be finishing up making the resin chess pieces. What are you working on John?"

"I have to file down the aluminum type used in making the laundry marking machines."

"Good, I want you to come over to me while emptying your filings and you will trip on the table leg spilling the filings in my work area. The guards will come running and become busy with cleaning up the floor while I scoop some of the filings into my resin. I will complain that my resin cannot be used because it has filings in it. While you and the guards are busy with the spill, I will place the caulk key mold into the waste collection cup and pour the resin in the cup and the mold. I will have put extra hardener in the mixture so very little time will be needed for the key to set up and harden. Upon throwing the waste cup out, I will palm the key and put it into my pocket. When we change our clothes from the shop attire, I will place the key into the toe of my shoe. Placing that finished key in the toe of my shoe will be such a relief from having that mold in the toe of my shoe," says Timothy.

"The guards pat us down on our way to the cell, but they never check our shoes. Isn't that strange, John?"

"Well, more the better for us, 'killer'."

"John, keep placing caulk in your shoe. We need it to fill in the mortar we take out from around the blocks in our cell."

"OK 'killer', but it ain't the color of the mortar."

"Come on John; you still are not thinking logically. We will mix the ground out mortar with the caulk, and it will look like mortar at a distance."

THE ESCAPE

J ohn and Tim are busy with the preparations for the escape. Tim thinks about Ronnie more and more every day. He sometimes calls her Julia in his dreams. The last time he went to see her for his blood test, she allowed him to touch her hand as he clasped his around hers. For a fleeting moment, Tim thought about divulging their escape plans to Ronnie so that she could go with him. He didn't know how that could happen or what he would say why he was escaping, now, instead of waiting for his release. It didn't matter; he was just as content fantasizing about it.

'Click' the lock on the infirmary door deactivates.

"All is clear, John. Ronnie is in the other room taking a phone call. Hurry up! Over there is the tool cabinet. Be sure to lock that door when you leave," Timothy whispers.

"I will, I will," says John.

"Ronnie is finished with her call and is coming back!" exclaims Timothy.

'Click' the lock on the infirmary door reactivates.

"Wow, Tim, what is wrong?" asks Ronnie. "You are sweating, and your face is all red."

"Those niacin vitamins gave me a buzz," answers Timothy. "How many pills did you take?" asks Ronnie.

"I took two like you told me before you went to answer the phone."

"No, Tim, you were to take two zinc pills and one niacin pill. Now, take another zinc pill. Your prostate will thank you," states Ronnie.

"Ronnie, what are you suggesting?" asks Timothy.

"Drink this water. It will help dissipate the niacin flush."

"As far as my concern for your prostate, the supplements I am giving you are for proper urinary tract flow, nothing else is intended!"

"Oh, I was just wondering, Ronnie."

RONNIE TURNS AROUND TO PLACE THE WATER GLASS ON THE COUNTER AND FOR A SECOND TIMOTHY THINKS OF JULIA WHILE GAZING AT RONNIE'S ASS

During Timothy's way back to his cell, he thinks how convenient it is to have the pills be the subject of his nervousness instead of the real cause; the close call involving John getting out of the infirmary. He takes the niacin pill from his pocket and swallows it. "There we go, one niacin pill and two zinc pills. Yup, just as Ronnie said."

"All is clear, 'killer.'"

"Good, just one more joint and these blocks are free. Tonight around midnight there is supposed to be a thunderstorm. John, how much lamp cord were you able to get from the machine shop?"

"I got about six feet worth."

"How did you manage that?"

"I told the guard that I needed it to make decorative knots. I even showed him one that I made. He would only allow me to take small pieces. You know, they are afraid that we might hang ourselves, or something."

"We will need to connect them. Also, John, you will need to get the guards to give you some ice. Make up some story."

"Yeah, sure 'killer', easier for you to say. Maybe I will tell them I have a toothache and then I can visit your girl in the infirmary. What's her name, 'killer'? Is it Ronnie?"

"John, you come up with some excuse for the ice, but it better not involve the infirmary. Ronnie is off limits to you."

"OK, the blocks are free, and we have the wrench. Now, cooperate mother nature, and give us a storm," Timothy prays.

IT IS THE NEXT AFTERNOON WHEN TIMOTHY'S PRAYERS ARE ANSWERED, AND A STORM ROLLS IN

"It must be a doozie of a storm, 'killer'. The lights are blinking and dimming. We haven't even started yet!"

"Get the ice ready, John."

JOHN HAS TALKED THE GUARD INTO GIVING HIM SOME ICE FOR HIS AILING 'STOMACHACHE'. HE TELLS THE GUARD THAT WHEN HIS ULCER ACTS UP, ICE IS THE ONLY THING THAT WILL CALM IT. THE GUARD THREATENS TO SEND HIM TO THE INFIRMARY, BUT JOHN REMEMBERS WHAT 'KILLER' HAD TOLD HIM AND PROCEEDS TO EXPLAIN TO THE GUARD THAT HE HAS ALREADY BEEN TO SEE THE NURSE AND ALL SHE DID IS SHOVE A THERMOMETER UP HIS ASS AND TOLD HIM TO SUCK ON SOME ICE. THE GUARD BUYS HIS STORY AND BRINGS HIM A LARGE BUCKET OF ICE.

"Now, John, hang that bed sheet on the cell bars. We don't want the other inmates in this hole to see what we are doing."

"Don't you think they will surmise something is going on when I hang the sheet?" John asks.

"No, they will think you, John, are a 'man' lover!" Timothy responds.

"Don't flatter me, 'killer'."

"I am not, you pig!"

Timothy removes a light bulb from the lighting fixture in his cell. He affixes the lamp cord to the light socket and the other end of the lamp cord to one of the steel bars behind the block wall to cause a short. "Now hold tight! Here goes!" Timothy exclaims.

"Damn, Timothy, that bar is red hot!"

"Quick, John, put that ice right here on the metal rod. OK, take it away and give the rod a heavy blow with your foot."

"Holy shit your idea works. That rod just snapped in half like it is made of wood!" John exclaims.

"Now we do the same thing to the other bar," states Timothy.

"Now hang that rag so that it can be shifted from inside the cell into the wall cavity," says Timothy. "Let's go over this. When you see a guard on rounds coming toward our cell, what do you do, John?"

"I shift this rag into the cavity so that you can see it and be alerted to get your ass back up here into the cell."

"Yes, and John, remember to give me enough time to get back into the cell, replace the blocks, fix the 'mortar' joints and push the sink back against the wall with bolts attached. When you see the guard come around the corner to our cell block, that is the time to alert me. There should be enough time for me to get back here and get everything back in place."

"Keep on the lookout, John. I am going down to the drainage pipe clean out and remove those bolts to the flange."

———

JOHN HUGS THE CELL BARS WITH THE MIRROR ADJUSTED SO THAT HE CAN SEE THE VERY END OF THE CELL BLOCK. HE IS CAREFUL TO NOT ALERT ANY INMATES ACROSS FROM HIS CELL BLOCK TO WHAT HE IS DOING. AFTER TIMOTHY CRAWLS THROUGH THE HOLE IN THE WALL AND FINDS THE LADDER HE REMEMBERS BACK WHEN HE WAS EIGHTEEN YEARS OLD, TO GET DOWN FROM THE STEAM PIPES TO THE MASSIVE DRAINAGE PIPE. HE THINKS BACK ON THE CONSTRUCTION PROJECT AND WONDERS WHY THE DESIGNERS OF THE DRAINAGE SYSTEM MADE THE PIPE SO LARGE, TWENTY-FOUR INCHES WOULD HAVE BEEN JUST FINE; EVEN EIGHTEEN INCHES

———

"Must be Karma. Somehow, it was decided that a large pipe was needed. Maybe the gods knew that I would need this large pipe to escape. They must have known that I would be in here, in this prison, sometime in my life," he mutters to himself.

Timothy crawls to the clean-out tee and loosens the flange bolts to remove the cover.

Timothy re-enters the cell.

———

"OK, John, we are all set. There isn't much water in the drainage pipe, but we will wait until tomorrow night for our escape."

"Just before 'lights out' John, I want you to start a ruckus with the inmates. The guards will be busy trying to stop it, and by the time they do, we will be on our way to freedom."

———

———

"John, it is 8:30 pm. I will make my way to the drainage pipe tee to check for water. When I get back, you are to start the ruckus. As soon as it is well underway, it will be about 8:55 pm."

———

TIMOTHY HASN'T RETURNED TO THE CELL. JOHN JUMPS THE GUN. HE
STARTS YELLING AT THE INMATES ACROSS FROM THEIR CELL

———

"Hey you 'dicks', you got any little girls or boys over there so I can play doctor? Oh, you don't? Well, I guess I can make an exception and play doctor with one of you!"

———

The inmates are angry, and one of them says, "Hey you big panty sniffer, wait until we get into the courtyard tomorrow, we will fix you so that you will never be able to play doctor again! We are going to chop your balls off!"

———

JOHN CONTINUES TO SHOOT INNUENDOS TO THE INMATES, AND ALL HELL
BREAKS LOOSE

———

"Guards to cell block B and make it fast. We have a mess on our hands. Toilet paper is thrown all over. The cons are clanging their cups across the bars and yelling. Hell, some of them are overturning their beds and throwing them against the bars," exclaims the Warden.

TIMOTHY EMERGES THROUGH THE OPENING IN THE WALL AND INTO THE CELL. THE RUCKUS THAT JOHN HAS STARTED IS WELL UNDERWAY

"John, I heard what you were saying, and you are disgusting! I wish that I hadn't needed you for this escape. You are not worth being free. Maybe we should delay our escape until the cons carry out their threat!"

"Now wait a minute, 'killer', you have skeletons in your closet too!"

"I don't ever want to hear you talk about your little fetish again! Is that clear?" Timothy exclaims with a question.

"Yeah, 'killer' whatever you say."

"Make sure that those beds look as if we are in them. Use the pillows and the clothes we are wearing."

"What? Why our clothes?" John asks.

"We have to remove all of our clothes except our undershorts. By spreading the baby oil all over our bare skin we will be able to slip through the drainage pipe much easier," Timothy says.

"How the hell are we going to get clothes when we get out? You know, it is winter out there!" exclaims John.

"Yup, but it is a warm winter at the moment. Remember, we just had a thunderstorm? We will get some clothes as soon as we get out."

"Don't you think the guards will notice we aren't in our beds?" asks John.

"By the time they discover we are gone, it will be close to morning, and we will be a good distance from here. We will get to Canada before they can catch up with us and then it will be too late. We will have blended in with society by then."

———

JOHN AND TIMOTHY CLIMB THROUGH THE HOLE IN THE CELL WALL AND CLIMB DOWN THE LADDER TO THE DRAINAGE PIPE. ABOUT FIFTY FEET ALONG THE PIPELINE IS THE CLEAN-OUT TEE

———

"John put the baby oil all over your bare skin and climb in that clean-out tee. Once in, you will turn to your right and then start crawling. I will be right behind you."

After crawling a distance, John asks Timothy.

"Where are we, 'killer'?"

"We have come to the central drainage system. We can now walk. See the stream of water and the direction that it is flowing? We have to go upstream to find the manhole we need for escape. If we go with the flow of water, we will end up in the lake."

"How far do we need to go? It feels like we have been in this sewer for at least two hours," says John.

"We have gone about five miles through this sewer system, and should be able to emerge from the next manhole we come upon."

"It is colder than hell, 'killer'. How about finding some clothes?"

"Keep walking. We will find some clothes."

"OK, this manhole should lead us to the street above," says Timothy.

"Hey, look, a gas station is down the road," states John.

They walk to the gas station and find a poorly locked door.

"We should be able to open the door without much force," states Timothy.

"Here, John, put these mechanics coveralls on."

"Look at this, John! I'll take this .38 caliber just in case we run into some wild animals on the trail," Timothy says amusingly.

"I am not interested in any use of a gun. We aren't planning on killing anyone, are we?" asks John.

"Remember John, we have escaped prison."

"Enough talk, we need to find the railroad. It will be our road to freedom," says Timothy.

CANTOR SQUARE

John and Timothy make their way through a field and come upon the railroad tracks.

"Which way are we going 'killer'?"

"We go north to Canada."

"I know, 'killer', but which way is north?"

"Look at the stars, John. We go in that direction; it is north."

"I am tired of walking these railroad tracks. I need some sleep. Let's find shelter and start again in the morning. We should be far away from the prison by now," says John.

"We are about sixty to seventy miles away from the border, I believe. If we keep on the railroad, we may be able to hitch a ride on a train going to Canada. It would be a great way to make up time," says Timothy.

"OK, here is a country road with very few houses. Let's cross this field and see what we can find," John says.

"John, we need to keep going. We need to create a long distance from that prison. They are sure to discover we are missing by now."

"Can't we at least wait until morning, 'killer'? My feet are killing me, and I am frozen to the bone. There isn't much darkness left before morning. We can start at the crack of dawn, but right now we need sleep."

"You are right, John. I am wicked tired myself. Let's see if we can find some shelter."

THEY TRUDGE THROUGH A FIELD ADJACENT TO THE RAILROAD TRACKS AND UP A COUPLE OF HILLS. THEY MAKE SURE THEY DON'T VENTURE TOO FAR FROM THE RAILROAD TRACKS

"That house appears vacant; we will spend the night and get some sleep," Timothy points.

"We will go to the second floor and find a room that overlooks the back of the house so we won't be seen by anyone."

THE TWO ENTER THE VACANT HOUSE AND MAKE THEIR WAY TO A BEDROOM, ON THE SECOND FLOOR, OVERLOOKING A LARGE HILL BEHIND THE HOUSE. BEFORE DOZING OFF TO SLEEP, JOHN STARTS A CONVERSATION WITH TIMOTHY

"OK, 'killer', what is with you and that chick from the infirmary? Are you going to try to hook up with her? I don't see how you can."

"Maybe," Timothy responds.

"Hey, you know, she reminds me of a broad that I knew."

"Oh, yeah, how so?" asks Timothy.

"Well, she had long beautiful black hair, tall and skinny, but shapely. She worked out or something. Her legs were the most beautifully sculpted that I have ever seen. She had the most beautiful face......"

"OK, enough about the broad John! I am too tired to get all excited about your description of her. Wait until morning and then you can tell me."

"All right, 'killer', but you could listen to me and have erotic dreams all night."

"Yeah, Yeah, Yeah," Timothy responds.

"Suit yourself, 'killer', suit yourself! I will have erotic dreams tonight," says John.

———

IT IS MID-MORNING BEFORE JOHN AND TIMOTHY WAKE UP FROM A RESTFUL SLEEP. ALTHOUGH IT IS LIGHT OUTSIDE, THE CLOUD COVER DOESN'T GIVE MUCH OF A CLUE OF THE TIME

———

"Before we get started, let me finish telling you about this broad I knew," says John.

"What is with you and this broad? Oh, I get it, I assume that she was a woman with small children, right John?"

"You think you have all the answers, 'killer'!"

"She did, but they weren't with her at the time. Now, let me tell you about her, it will invigorate your system like a cup of coffee, of which we do not have."

"OK, OK, John, but you need to start from the beginning. I forgot the first part of the story you were blabbering last night, or whatever time it was."

"Well, she had long beautiful black hair, tall and skinny, but shapely. She worked out or something. Her legs were the most

111

beautifully sculpted that I have ever seen. She had the most beautiful face, almond eyes and little dimples on her cheeks and her ass; well, her ass was worth visiting more than once."

"So, why are you telling me this?" asks Timothy.

"Because I was just thinking about the broad at the infirmary, your girl, when you were describing her looks to me; it stirred me sexually and reminded me of this broad I am describing."

"You see, this woman I am describing was the most sexually active and satisfying cunt that I have ever fucked. Once she wrapped her legs around me, pure ecstasy flowed throughout my whole body."

"The poor bastard of a husband she had, didn't know I was fucking her, and how she moaned every time I penetrated her ass."

"Wait a minute, John. Did she ever mention her husband?"

"No way! The indication that I had; he was a loser, the jealous type. She was good at being discreet about us, though."

"John, what was her name?" Timothy asks with agitation.

"I think I remember that her name was Jenna or something like that. I know it started with the letter 'J'."

"Are you sure her name wasn't Julia?"

"Oh, hell, I don't know. What would the name matter? She might have said that her name was like that. Maybe, Julie, I don't remember her name; just her ass!"

"You bastard, John! You dirty panty sniffing, dick sucking bastard! You! You!"

"What the hell are you doing, 'killer'? Why are you pointing that gun at me?"

"I am going to kill you, you prick! You are the one who was fucking my wife, Julia! You described her exactly!"

"Wait a minute 'killer'. How do you know that for sure?"

"I know, I know, it all fits and I am going to kill you!"

"Well, 'killer', maybe so. You know, she fucked like a machine. She would..."

Blam! Blam! Blam!

JOHN FELL TO THE FLOOR DEAD, AND A POOL OF BLOOD IMMEDIATELY
SURROUNDED HIM. THE BULLETS WENT CLEAN THROUGH AND RIGHT INTO
THE WALL BEHIND HIM

———

THE HILL

It was a great day for sledding, and it was Saturday. Tony and John contemplate going across the street to go sledding, but they feel much more adventurous today.

"Hey, let's go up to that house that is across the street from Highland's house. We can sled down the huge hill," suggests Tony.

"OK, but let's go through the field instead of up the road. You never know what we may find," says John.

"Yeah, maybe there are some good finds on the railroad tracks," says Tony.

"Hey John, take a look at these footprints in the snow. They start here, at the railroad tracks, and go up through the field exactly the way we are going to the big hill," says Tony.

"The footprints look rather fresh, and there are two sets of them. I wonder who they belong to," ponders John.

"The house looks vacant," says Tony.

"I wonder if anyone is living in it," John interjects.

"Maybe the tracks belong to the people who own it, although it looks like no one lives there. Do you think we should go in and see?" asks Tony.

"No, no, we can't. I don't want to. Remember the hermit scare we had at school a year ago before our summer vacation? I heard that they never found the hermit. Sure was scary! Remember, they swore that the hermit kidnapped Wanda," says John.

"Who was Wanda?"

"You know, the girl in school who didn't wear underpants."

"What are you talking about?" asks Tony.

"Never mind. Wanda was found later. The story has it her father came to pick her up from the playground and the school did not know, and they thought that the hermit took her," says John.

"Shh, John, I hear voices coming from the house. Whoever they are, it sounds like they are arguing and it sounds like they are upstairs."

"I..I..don't want to go in," says John as he stutters, "What if one of them is the hermit they never found. Suppose he is a kidnapper?"

"We can't slide down the hill, now. They might see us. Let's get ought of here!" exclaims Tony.

AS THE TWO BOYS EXIT THE PROPERTY, THEY SEE A POLICE HELICOPTER HOVERING THE AREA AND HEAR, IN THE DISTANCE OF THE RAILROAD TRACKS, THE HOWLING OF DOGS. ALL OF A SUDDEN THEY HEAR BLAM! BLAM! BLAM! THE SOUND WAS COMING FROM THE DIRECTION OF THE HOUSE

MANHUNT

The Warden at the Jackson City Prison wants answers.

"How the hell did those two escape from my prison?" asks the Warden.

"We are not exactly sure, Warden. We are trying to piece it together," says one of the guards.

"I want the lead guard of cell block one, nurse Ronnie and the night patrol guard in my office immediately. I also want the records for last nights rounds and camera footage of the hall leading to the infirmary," orders the Warden.

THE MEETING THE WARDEN CALLS IS ABOUT TO GET UNDERWAY JUST AS
THE COMMISSIONER PLACES HIS CALL TO THE JACKSON CITY PRISON

"Commissioner, we are working to piece the details of this escape together. As soon as we make headway, I will be in contact with you," the Warden promises.

"Charlie what have you found in the cell of John Bailey and Timothy Lillus?" asks the Warden.

"Warden, a hole was cut through the wall behind the sink by removing two concrete blocks. They climbed down to the drainage pipe and crawled through it. I suppose that once they crawled to the main sewer, they could go just about anywhere they wanted and probably exited via a manhole somewhere."

"Charlie, steel bars are lining the cell walls just behind the block walls. How did they get through them?" asks the Warden.

"I do not know how, but they are broken. By the looks of the breaks on the bars, it appears that they were snapped."

"Jim, at what time was 'lights out'?" asks the Warden.

"If you remember, Warden, last night around 8:55 pm, there was a huge ruckus in cell block one, two, three, and four. It appears it was started by the pedophile John Bailey stirring up trouble calling out innuendoes. It took a bit of time to get those cell blocks quieted down. I believe we finally had lights out at around 9:30 pm. My inspection patrol started at cell block four, and they worked their way down to cell block one. It appeared that both John and Timothy were in their cell at that time. This morning it was discovered the bundled clothing and pillows were making the appearance of those two in their beds."

"What clothes did they wear?" asks the Warden.

"I am not sure about that, because their prison outfits were left behind, but we did find an empty bottle of baby oil in their cell. There was a prescription written from the infirmary."

"Nurse Ronnie, what details do you have and why the baby oil?" asks the Warden.

"Well, sir, I am confused why Timothy Lillus escaped when he was going to be released in a couple of weeks."

"Where did you get that from, Ronnie? He was in no way going to be released," states the Warden.

"Timothy Lillus was under my care because he needed his blood sugar levels tested each week. He has diabetes. He told me that he was here because they convicted him of murdering his wife, but later it was found he was wrongly accused, and they found the guy who killed his wife."

"That isn't true, Ronnie. Timothy murdered his wife and his wife's best friend. Did you know that Timothy Lillus is said to have Pathological Jealousy Affliction?" asks the Warden.

"No, I did not know that, and he painted a pretty convincing story about his wife's murder. He was very sly making a pass at me claiming that I reminded him of his wife. He even wanted to take me to dinner when he was released. How foolish I was to believe a con!"

"It appears, Ronnie, that he dazed you with his charm to get your guard down. We found a resin key infused with aluminum filings exhibiting the same characteristics as the infirmary key. They needed tools to escape, and they must have gotten the tools from the cabinet in the infirmary," says the Warden.

"Somehow, Timothy must have gotten my key to the infirmary and made a resin key. It must have been when I left the examining room to get the bottle of baby oil for his skin. He has dehydrated skin," says Ronnie.

"We found the key mold in the trash can located in the shop. We also found hardened resin infused with aluminum filings. I still am puzzled why the bottle of baby oil was empty when you dispensed it just two days ago," ponders the Warden.

"I have a theory, Warden," says Charlie.

"What is it, Charlie?"

"I was wondering what that greasy, oily residue was on the floor near the entrance to the drain pipe and why the same residue is on the inside of the clean-out tee. It must be the baby oil. I would venture to guess those two stripped down and spread the baby oil over their bodies to make it easier to slide through the drain pipe. It would also explain why they left their clothes in the cell."

"I am still puzzled when they entered the infirmary to grab the tools from the cabinet and not be seen," ponders the Warden.

"Warden, if I were to venture a guess, it is because there are no cameras in the hall where the infirmary door is located. John Bailey was the mobile librarian, and I would suppose with the correct timing, he could unlock the door to the infirmary and grab the tools from the cabinet, while Timothy was waiting for me to get the baby oil for his dehydrated skin condition. He could then slip them in a book and pass the book to his partner, Timothy Lillus at their cell," Ronnie explains.

"Warden."

"What is it, Jim?"

"We checked the tapes for the past week and noticed that at one time John Bailey dropped some books from his cart while traveling past the infirmary door. It took about five minutes between the time he dropped the books and was out of camera view and then back in camera view at the other end of the hall to the infirmary. With some precision, I suppose John could have been able to open the infirmary door and take the tools from the cabinet. He could re-lock the door and place the tools in the books to be passed to his partner within the five-minute window. The guards wouldn't think anything fishy because they saw John had dropped the books. They would understand the lapse of time before he showed up in the next camera."

"Excuse me Warden, there is an important call for you. I believe they have found a possible location of those two escaped convicts," the receptionist interrupts.

"Thank you, Kimberly."

"Warden?" asks a guard who had joined the manhunt.

"Yes, this is the Warden."

"We feel we have located the two escapees. The dogs are following a good scent, and we see tracks in the snow. Funny though, we see two adult footprints and two youth-sized footprints."

"I sure hope they haven't taken hostages. Where are those footprints?" asks the Warden.

"They are in a field in Canton Square, and they appear to be going straight to what appears to be a vacant house."

"OK, that area is the Harford Police territory. I will give them a call for back up."

"Chief Roland?"

"Yes, this is Roland."

"This is Warden Smith from the Jackson City Prison, and we are tracking two escapees. We have found a trail in your territory up in Canton Square."

"How far away are you from apprehending those two escapees?"

"I am told the footprints and the dogs are heading to a vacant house. We are at the bottom of the hill at the moment and are awaiting your input," says the Warden.

"I will dispatch two deputies immediately. Please do not approach the vacant house until my deputies get on site."

"OK, Chief Roland, we will wait for you."

"Peltz, take Angel with you, and head to Canter Square. The Warden at the prison thinks they have found those two escaped convicts, John Bailey and Timothy Lillus, from Jackson City. I have ordered them to wait until you arrive before apprehension. Please be careful out there. Those two may be armed," says Chief Roland.

OFFICER PELTZ AND OFFICER ANGEL GET INTO THE PATROL CAR AND HEAD FOR CANTON SQUARE

"Angel, I see no Officers or dogs. Are we at the correct address?" asks Officer Peltz.

"They must be on the other side of the hill. I purposely came the back way to not raise suspicion in case those escapees are watching," says Angel.

AS ANGEL STEPS OUT OF THE PATROL CAR, SHE HEADS TOWARD THE DOOR OF THE VACANT HOUSE

"I am going in."

"No, you are not Angel. Not by yourself!" exclaims Officer Peltz.

"Look, you are my back-up. I am going in, and you hang back!" exclaims Angel.

"It sounds pretty quiet in here, but I think that I heard some movement coming from the second floor," whispers Officer Peltz, "Do you think they know we are here?"

"I don't know, Peltz. Just stay behind me."

"Angel, please be careful. You remember what the Chief had said about them possibly being armed."

"I am good, Peltz. I will be careful."

ANGEL AND PELTZ ASCEND THE OLD STAIRS AND SEE TWO BEDROOMS ON THE SECOND FLOOR. ONE BEDROOM HAS A DOOR THAT IS SHUT

"They are behind that closed door. I will crash the door with a gun in hand. You stay back by the stairs, Peltz, in case they have a gun and fire on me. No need for you to get hit by a stray bullet."

"But, what about you Angel?"

"This is the Harford Police! I am armed and suggest you drop your weapon and let me in. If you don't let me in, I will crash this door. Now open it! One - two - three," Angel kicks the door open.

"What?.......What the hell!" exclaims Timothy.

"Timothy Lillus, drop your weapon!" hollers Angel.

Blam! Blam!

ANGEL FALLS BACK, HITS THE WALL TO THE BEDROOM, AS SHE SLUMPS TO THE FLOOR AND HER GUN SLIPS OUT OF HER HAND OFFICER PELTZ ENTERS THE ROOM, SEES ANOTHER MAN LYING ON THE FLOOR IN A POOL OF COAGULATED BLOOD, WITH THREE BULLET HOLES IN HIS CHEST. NEXT TO THE DOOR SLUMPED ON THE FLOOR NEAR THE WALL LIES ANGEL, LIFELESS. TIMOTHY IS NOWHERE IN SIGHT

"Oh my God! Angel is down!"

"Angel, Angel! Oh my God, I think she is dead," as Officer Peltz carefully rolls her on her back.

"Come on, Angel! Don't die on me!"

OFFICER PELTZ REACHES DOWN CAREFULLY PARTING HER HAIR FROM IN FRONT OF HER FACE. HE PLACES HIS EAR RIGHT OVER ANGEL'S MOUTH

"Oh, God! I can't feel any breath! Angel! You can't die on me! Please, honey, wake up," as he caresses her forehead with his hand.

ANGEL SURVIVES

"Chief, this isPeltz. Angel has been shot and I am not sure if she is alive. I don't think she is breathing."

"Peltz, what the hell happened?"

"Chief, Angel insisted on storming the door where Timothy and the other guy were holding out, and it appears Timothy Lillus shot her."

"Where is Timothy?"

"I don't know, he wasn't in the room when I went in and discovered Angel had been shot. The other guy had been shot, I presume by Timothy, and slumped over dead on the floor."

"Peltz, how is Angel? Did you call an ambulance?"

"Yes, Chief, I called right away and when they arrived, they didn't tell me much and just took her away to the emergency room. I am on my way to see how she is doing…or if she is still alive."

"Angel, are you OK?" asks Peltz.

"I am doing OK, Peltz. Unfortunately the bullet hit the edge of my body armor and lodged in my side. If it not hit the body armor, I probably wouldn't be here; the bullet would have much deeper."

"Did you see Timothy ?"

"Peltz, I saw a flash of him running as I hit the floor and then I was out for the count."

"I know Angel, I thought you were dead. I couldn't feel your breath."

"Well, Peltz, I am here. You can't get rid of me that quickly."

THE DISCOVERY

T here is a knock on Chief Roland's office door.

"Come in...what? How in the hell? Julia! We thought that you were dead. We looked all over for your body. What happened? Are you all right?"

"Timothy stabbed me, and I thought that I wouldn't make it. I passed out. How is Amanda?"

"She..well, we found her in the car we pulled from the creek. I am so sorry, Julia. I know how much of a good friend she was to you."

"Timothy stabbed her to death because she witnessed Timothy stabbing you. Were you in the car too?"

"I don't know. When I came to, I found myself floating down the river. Thank God the garbage bag I was wrapped in was mostly torn off or I would have drowned."

"So what happened? Where did you go and how?"

"I was finally able to pull myself to shore and hobble to the nearest home I could find."

—Julia pulls herself from the river and realizes that she is nude and cold. She is wounded badly from the stab wounds inflicted on her by Timothy. She slowly crawls to the door and knocks. As soon as the door opens, Julia says, "Help me…help me…," with labored breath.

"Henry, get a blanket and pass it to me. Don't come over here to the door."

"You poor dear! Here, let me wrap this blanket around you."

"Henry, come here and help me. This poor girl is injured bad. She needs to go to the ER."

"Honey, we are going to take you to the hospital. No, don't try to talk. You rest. Everything is going to be OK."

"Henry, warm up the truck and turn up the heater. This poor dear is shivering. All she has for clothes is this blanket I have her wrapped in. I do not know where her clothes are. Hurry, Henry. She has lost a lot of blood, and she is dying. I can see the life slowly draining from her face. She is such a beautiful girl."

"No, honey, please do not try to talk. Save your energy. We are almost to the hospital."—

"I guess when they saw me, they knew I had to get to the ER to survive the stab wounds."

"While in the ER, I heard the doctor tell the nurse it was a miracle I was still alive. Those stab wounds just about killed me. I lost a lot of blood."

"I stayed in the hospital a week. I was in no hurry to get out because I did not know if Timothy was still out there. If he saw me alive, I would have had no second chance of living."

"What did you do then?"

"I went to my sister's house in Constantia. She is abroad, so no one knew I was there. I then saw on the television that Timothy was in prison and felt it was safe to leave the house, but I was not ready to come back, here, to my job."

"I am glad that you didn't! Are you OK now?"

"Yes, Chief; a little weak, but OK," states Julia.

"Chief, I want to go and get Timothy and Bailey now that they have been located since their escape."

"Are you sure, Julia? After all that has happened. I sent Peltz and Angel to get them and Angel was shot, apparently by Timothy," states the Chief.

"Is she OK?"

"I am not sure, Julia. Peltz went to the emergency room to be with her," says the Chief.

"I want to go and get him!" exclaims Julia.

He is probably armed, and if he sees you, it could be the last that I see you."

"I will be careful. I will be right back. I am going to freshen-up in the ladies room."

––––––––

"Hey, Peltz, how is Angel?" asks the Chief.

"She is going to survive, thanks to her body armor......"

"Hey, what? Julia!"

"Hello, Peltz."

"So how...?"

"I will fill you in later Peltz. Right now I have work to do."

"From now on, I am calling you an angel because you have got to be an angel to escape death the way that you have. We knew you were in the submerged car with Amanda because we found strands of your hair in there," states Peltz.

"Come on Richard, let's go get those guys. I need you for my back-up. Timothy Lillus and John Bailey need to be brought back to prison where they belong, especially Tim!"

"Just so you know, the other guy, Bailey? Well, he is dead," states Richard Peltz.

THE SHOOTING

The vacant house is now a house of horrors. Death is felt in every corner. An Officer has been shot, and it is not known where Timothy Lillus is.

Outside the bedroom door where Richard told Julia Timothy was last seen, Julia draws her gun.

"Timothy Lillus, I know you are in there. Come out with your hands up and no one will be hurt!" exclaims Julia.

Richard immediately grabs Julia by the arm and pulls her away from the door just in time to avoid the bullets fired into the door from Timothy's gun. Julia kicks the door open with gun in hand.

"What…what?" Timothy gasps in question.

"Drop it, Timothy!" exclaims Julia.

Timothy quickly raises his gun as he fires at Julia. Julia returns fire, but too late. She immediately slumps to the floor as Timothy's bullet hits her square in the chest.

Timothy lies on the floor, blood pouring out of a wound in his chest.

"Julia! Julia! Are you with me? Are you injured?"

"Yeah, no; Peltz, give me a few minutes. Help me up."

"Sweet Jesus! I thought that I had lost you!"

PELTZ HELPS JULIA TO HER FEET, AND WRAPS HIS ARMS AROUND HER AND HUGS HER

"Careful Peltz. Let me recover!"

Peltz releases Julia; he feels the strong urge to kiss her.

He then, pulls Julia gently to him, and he aligns his lips to her ear, and says, "Honey, I cannot bear the thought of losing you."

"I'm all right, now, Peltz."

"It looks like the other guy has been laying there for a while. The pool of blood surrounding him is coagulated," states Peltz.

"Yes, it appears that Tim shot and killed him before we got here. Tim has a .38 caliber in his hands, and by the look of the bullet holes in the wall behind that guy, Tim shot him."

"Julia, do you have any idea who that guy is?"

"I believe the guy lying there, dead, goes by the name of John Bailey."

"There were two shots fired, and by the looks of it, one of those shots was yours. Why did you shoot Timothy?"

"I didn't want too, and I certainly was not thinking at the time, to fire a lethal shot. As soon as I crossed through the doorway into the bedroom, Tim lifted his gun and pointed it at me. I wanted to talk to him, but it was too late. He shot at me when the expression on his face 'spelled my name'. I fired back. I didn't come here to kill Tim, but as it worked out, I didn't want to see Tim returned to prison either. I just wanted him entirely out of my life!"

OFFICER PELTZ PUTS HIS ARM AROUND JULIA AS SHE WEEPS. HE NOTICES
JULIA IS STILL VERY WEAK FROM THE WOUND THAT TIMOTHY INFLICTED
UPON HER

"Julia, you did what you had to. No one can fault you for that."

"I know Richard, but in some way, and I don't know why, I still love Tim, in spite of what he has done. He was a very sick man."

"Yes, Julia, he was a very sick man. I know how much you loved Timothy and always wished that he would get well. The important thing now is that you are still alive and you will be OK."

HER EXPLANATION

A cross-examination by Chief Roland is in progress with Officer Peltz and Officer Julia Lillus at the police station.

———————

"Tell me, Julia, did Timothy fire at you when you entered the bedroom?" asks Chief Roland.

"I warned before I entered. I crashed through the door when Tim wouldn't open it. As soon as I entered the room, I saw John Bailey, dead, on the floor in a pool of blood. It looked like he had been lying there dead, for some time. Tim's expression on his face was that of great surprise when he saw my face. He undoubtedly thought for sure that he had killed me that night in our home, got scared and shot directly into my chest. That is when I fired back at him."

"It was good thinking on your part, you put your Kevlar® on before you went to apprehend him."

"Chief, I never leave home without it," Julia says smiling.

"Julia, you have been through a lot the past few weeks. I have asked Officer Fritz if it will be all right for you to stay with her until you are strong enough to go back to your home. Bobbie told me that you are welcome to stay as long as you like."

"Thank you, Chief. I don't think that I could be at my home and face all of the memories I had made with Tim. In spite of what all has happened and what everyone may think, I loved Tim very much, and I poured my life into our relationship. Tim was a good man, but he was sick."

JULIA FIGHTS WITH HER EMOTIONS, BUT SHE CANNOT STOP THE TEARS RUNNING DOWN HER CHEEKS.
CHIEF ROLAND REACHES OVER AND WRAPS HIS HAND CAREFULLY AROUND JULIA'S HAND

"Oh, Frank, I am so sorry. It is so hard for me," Julia says weeping.

"I know, honey. We all know."

"Bobbie will be here any minute. Please go with her and rest. I do not want to see you back here until you are ready. OK, Julia?"

CHIEF ROLAND LEANS OVER THE DESK AND KISSES JULIA ON THE CHEEK

"OK, Chief and thank you for everything that you have done for me. I appreciate it."

"No problem, any time, angel, and I mean you are an angel!"

SECOND LOVE

It has been several weeks, and Julia is thinking of returning to work at the Police Station. She continues to stay at Bobbie's home. Julia has no desire to visit her home. She had Bobbie go over and get her clothes from her bedroom closet. It hurts too much for Julia to think of the times Tim and she would make love, and going into their bedroom and facing their bed would bring all of those memories back to life, except this time they will be shattered. Julia cannot bear the thought of the shattering of those memories.

"Bobby, thanks so much for allowing me to stay with you at your home," says Julia.

"It is my pleasure, Julia. I want you to know there is no time limit for your stay with me."

"Oh, thank you so much Bobbie. I will start looking for a place to stay once I feel up to it. I am very appreciative to you for going to my home and getting my clothes for me. I couldn't face going into that house with all the memories of Tim and my relationship. It would hurt too much. I don't think I can ever go back to my home."

"Honey, you can stay with me as long as you need."

"Bobbie, I know the feelings you have for Richard Peltz."

"Yes, I like him very much, but......"

"I know. It has become more apparent since this case has come to a close. I feel Richard has more feelings for me than just a partner at work. When the two of us were in that vacant house, and I was lying on the floor, unconscious from the blow of Tim's bullet, I sensed that Richard was getting very emotionally involved with me. Don't get me wrong, I am thankful for Richard caring so much for me when he thought I might be dead, but at one instance I felt he wanted to kiss me. It wasn't just a kiss, but a passionate in-love kiss."

"Now, Julia, in case you did't know, which I think you do in some way, Richard has had a crush on you ever since you became part of the Police Department. I know this because I have heard conversations he has had with others that blatantly proved his infatuation with you. I can't say that I blame him. You are a beautiful woman."

"Come on, Bobbie. I am just an ordinary female."

"Because of Richard's infatuation with you, he has not been able to see how much I am infatuated with him."

"Bobbie, I hope that you know I have never purposely done anything to allure him to me. I would never have done such a thing because I loved Tim and I poured my heart and soul into our relationship."

"I do know that, Julia. I was not inferring that at all. I know how hard you worked on your relationship with Tim."

"Bobbie, I don't know what I can do to change Richard's affection for me, but I must ask of you...."

"Julia, I tried, and I tried to no avail."

"Bobbie, we can work on this together, but I need you to work hard on steering Richard away from me."

"I do not wish to have a relationship with Richard or any man, for that matter. It is quite obvious that I wouldn't be interested in a platonic relationship at this time. If I were truthful to my feelings, Bobbie, I don't think anyone could replace what I had with Tim. He was sick, but in-between all of that, he was a very loving man, and Tim loved me dearly. I do not feel that I will ever get over this to allow another man into my life."

"I understand Julia. What can I do to direct Richard's attention away from you long enough for him to be able to recognize my feelings for him?"

"The first thing that I will be asking the Chief when I get back to work is to request that you and Richard become work partners."

"But, what about you, Julia? Who would be your partner?"

"I am not going to worry about that at the moment. Besides, it will be a while until I am ready to get back out in the field to work. There will be plenty of time for Richard and you to become partners."

"That sounds like a good start, Julia."

"Bobbie, the priority in my mind, is to get Richard's emotional infatuation away from me. The second is a wish Richard can build a relationship with you. It would be good for both of you."

WHY?

J ulia has gained enough strength physically and emotionally to
start work at the Harford Police Department.

"Julia, it is nice to see you. How are you feeling?"

"I am OK, Chief. I am learning to get along with my life without
Tim."

"How is it working out for you at Bobbie's home?"

"Chief, she is a godsend. She is so sweet, and we hit it off very well.
She isn't pressuring me to leave, but I know that I will need to find an
apartment soon. She needs to have her life without me interfering."

"I am sure that she doesn't feel that way. I can't see where you
could ever interfere in anyone's life, Julia."

"Chief, why do I feel you are hitting on me?" Julia asks with a
smile.

"Oh, no no, I wouldn't think of it cupcake."

"Chief!"

"Julia, would it be OK if I ask you a few questions that have
puzzled me ever since this whole mess started?"

"Please stop me if it becomes too unbearable."

"Sure, Chief, I think that I can handle it, but I have a request to ask of you."

"Sure, Julia, you can ask me anything."

"Richard has an infatuation with me, and I understand that he has for a long time. It's not Richard so much, but, Chief, I am not ready to enter into a relationship with a man at this time. You know the feelings I had and still have for Tim. I don't think that I will ever feel the need to enter into a relationship with a man, again."

"I am asking that you pair up Richard with Bobbie instead of me. I probably won't feel up to going out in the field in deep cases for a while. I can take Bobbie's cases of family personality differences and disputes."

"Sure, Julia, whatever you want. You do know that I feel you are a hell of an Officer and you flourish your best in those deep cases, but I will honor your request, at least for a while. I have plans for you, cupcake!"

"OK, Chief, I do not think that I can take two hits on me in a single day!"

"Seriously, Julia, and I mean it when I say I am serious about this. You are the best Officer that I have ever had work with me and I truly am so thankful for you! If you only knew how much agony I went through; the entire police force, when you were missing and possibly dead. It is why I call you 'cupcake'. It is the only way I know of to express my extreme gratitude for all you have done for this Department and the vast appreciation I have in knowing you as a close friend, without invading your space."

JULIA STANDS UP FROM HER CHAIR AND WALKS OVER TO THE OTHER SIDE OF THE DESK WHERE THE CHIEF IS SITTING. JULIA BENDS DOWN TO HIM

"There you go, Chief. I hope you do not mind that I have invaded your space," as she places her lips on his cheek and kisses him.

"Julia, why do you think that Timothy did this to you?" asks the Chief.

"Tim was a very jealous man. He was diagnosed with Pathological Jealousy Affliction, or Othello's Syndrome, as they also call it. He and I knew of this for many years. His case was typical, and the affliction got worse over time. He was convinced I was having an affair. I loved Tim dearly and was very happy with him. I believe deep down in his heart he knew I loved him deeply. His jealousy at first, was an adhesive element to our marriage because it made me feel I was special to him and he wanted to be with me. But, as time advanced, the jealousy got more intense and crazy to the point of mistrusting me and conjuring up affairs that I never had. He couldn't trust me when I went to the gym or anywhere without him. When we were together in public, he would 'see' other men making passes at me that never existed. It got so that an argument would erupt every time I was out, accusing me of alluring men to myself because of my appearance. Tim would always tell me how beautiful I was to him, but he couldn't get past his fear of believing that all the other men in the world could think the same way and that they could steal me from him. It eventually led to him not being able to overcome his fears and probably lead him no choice but to get rid of me by killing me. I am sure that if his mind were right, he would have never thought of harming or murdering me. He must have killed Amanda because she saw what he had done to me. Amanda dropped me off at my home that night after our exercise routine at the gym. I had asked her to always wait a minute or two until I entered the house just in case Tim started an argument. I was afraid, that night, Tim would harm me. He was outraged, but it wasn't displayed to the extreme for me to fear him until after Amanda had left for her home. I managed to escape to the bathroom and call Amanda to come back and help me. Amanda did not pick up her phone, so I left a desperate message. She got my message too late. By the time she arrived at my home, Tim had already stabbed me and left me for dead. Amanda was such a protective friend. As I said, she always waited to see if I got into my home safely before she drove away. She also knew about Tim's jealous nature because I discussed it with her. So, that night, there was an argument, but way after Amanda left. Poor Amanda, she did not deserve to die."

"So, how does John Bailey fit into this puzzle?" asks the Chief.

"I don't know, but I feel that whatever transpired between Tim and him, had something to do with Tim's jealousy. It is possible that Tim thought John Bailey was somehow connected to me. Maybe he felt that John was the person who was having an affair with me or 'had to be the one' having an affair with me to qualify his jealousy."

"Julia, in case you didn't know, John Bailey was a pedophile. He used his charm on mothers with small children in order get close to them, and you know what happens then."

"Yes, Chief, it is disgusting."

"During the trial that convicted John Bailey, it was brought out he bragged about a certain woman with whom he was having an affair. It just so happens this woman could have been your twin."

"Oh my God, I bet that John Bailey bragged about the affair with that woman to Tim," states Julia.

"It's possible it was the case. Those two shared a cell at the prison. John probably didn't brag to Timothy until they holed up in that house in Canton Square."

"I don't know, Chief. No telling what runs through the mind of a man fearing and imagining affairs due to his jealousy."

OTHELLO'S SYNDROME:

I t is the delusion of infidelity of a spouse or partner. The Othello
syndrome affects males and, less often, females. It is characterized by
recurrent accusations of infidelity, searches for evidence, repeated
interrogation of the partner, tests of their partner's fidelity, and sometimes
stalking. The syndrome may appear by itself or in the course of
paranoid schizophrenia, alcoholism, or cocaine addiction. As in Othello, the
play by Shakespeare, the syndrome can be highly dangerous and result in
disruption of a marriage, homicide, and suicide.

The Othello syndrome was named by the English psychiatrist John Todd
(1914-1987) in a paper he published with K. Dewhurst entitled "The Othello
Syndrome: a study in the psychopathology of sexual jealousy" (Journal of
Nervous and Mental Disorder, 1955, 122: 367). Todd was also the first to
name the Alice in Wonderland syndrome.

The Othello syndrome is also known as delusional jealousy, erotic
jealousy syndrome, morbid jealousy, Othello psychosis, or sexual jealousy.

—Taken from MedicineNet—

EPILOGUE

Fter the trial, Sara Dowd slowly healed from her assault with the help of a counselor specializing in those who have been victims of sexual assault due to pedophilia, both children and adults. Sara has vowed to commit herself to study in helping parents recognize symptoms displayed by child victims and how to stop the advent of the rape and expose the pedophile.

The boys continued to travel to that big hill to slide after the vacant house was torn down. The stories about the incident continued to be embellished each year when they told it to their class, and somehow, the hermit was always mentioned in part of the story.

Was it true that Wanda did not wear underpants when at school? Those boys!

The hermit was never real. He was a person the class made up to feed their fears. Imagination at that age is such a good virtue.

Officer Richard Peltz continued to be an asset to the Harford Police Department with his new partner, Officer Bobbie Fritz.

Officer Bobbie Fritz also continued to be an asset to the Harford Police Department. Over time, Bobbie was able to shift Richard Peltz's infatuation that he had for Julia to herself. They expect to be married next year.

Chief Roland retired within the year and traveled the world with his wife.

John Bailey was buried in the Jackson City Prison Cemetery, and no one visited his grave.

Timothy Lillus was buried in the Cloverville Cemetery. Julia often visited his grave, and if one passed by, they would hear her asking, "Why?" as she sobbed.

Amanda was buried in the Canter Square cemetery and tears of sadness flowed from the eyes of all those who visited her grave. Julia always brought flowers drenched in her tears.

Julia wasn't interested in starting a new relationship with a man and never moved back into her home. She became an asset to the Harford Police Department as the new Chief.

The child victims of pedophilia have become more aware of the assault and are beginning to realize that it is not their fault. They are seeking help by reaching out and when approached. More and more pedophiles are being stopped in their heinous and grotesque acts before they can assault more children. All of this is due to those that are willing to come forward, and the successfully tried cases in the court systems.

And finally, jealousy, of any kind, especially the Pathological Jealousy Affliction, or Othello's Syndrome, is a dead end. It robs your spirit, your marriage, your relationships and your ability to love in trust.

ABOUT THE AUTHOR

James Roberts is an emerging author of Murder, Erotic Sex, and Deceit. The reader is challenged by the experiences seen through the eyes of his characters, and although fiction in nature, allows the reader to experience real-life situations relatable to their world, and invites the reader to explore their inner feelings of right and wrong based on those experiences.

This is Book One of A Julia Lillus Series of adult books written by James Roberts.